Dire Distraction

Dire Distraction

DEE DAVIS

New York Boston

Copyright © 2013 by Dee Davis Oberwetter
Excerpt from *Dark Deceptions* copyright © 2010 by Dee Davis Oberwetter
Cover design by Diane Luger. Cover copyright © 2013 by Hachette Book Group, Inc.

Forever Yours
Hachette Book Group
237 Park Avenue, New York, NY 10017
www.hachettebookgroup.com
www.twitter.com/foreverromance

First published as an e-book and as a print on demand edition: June 2013
Forever Yours is an imprint of Grand Central Publishing.

The Forever Yours name and logo are trademarks of Hachette Book Group, Inc.
The publisher is not responsible for websites (or their content) that are not owned by the publisher.

The Hachette Speakers Bureau provides a wide range of authors for speaking events. To find out more, go to www.hachettespeakersbureau.com or call (866) 376-6591.

ISBN 978-1-4555-7368-4 (e-book edition)
ISBN 978-1-4555-7530-5 (print on demand edition)

In Memory of Max

Best. Dog. Ever.

Dire Distraction

Prologue

Koln, Germany

Michael Brecht twisted the browning rose bloom, snapping it off the plant. He'd been thwarted by A-Tac, again. It was as if Avery Solomon was always there, looking over his shoulder, waiting to swoop in at the last minute in his goddamned white hat.

It had taken months to coordinate the events leading up to the assassination attempt on Bilaal Hamden, and only seconds for A-Tac to ruin everything. All that hard work—and nothing to show for it. Michael grabbed another stem, popping the dead flowers off the rose bush with a zeal that went beyond deadheading. He'd made his plans so carefully. Every detail checked and rechecked. Even when things had gotten out of hand, he'd managed to maintain control, only to lose everything when it had mattered most.

A thorn dug into his thumb, and he swore, sucking away the blood as someone behind him cleared his throat.

Gregor.

Michael stifled a sigh and turned around, surprised to see that his number two was not alone. Anthony Delafranco was supposed to be in Nice. The Consortium had business there. Delafranco, one of the Consortium's founding members, was supposed to have been on point.

"Is there a problem?" Michael asked, his senses on high alert. A second man—armed—stood behind Delafranco. Michael recognized him as Delafranco's bodyguard. Nothing unusual in that, but something felt off somehow.

"Nothing that we can't handle," Delafranco replied, his expression guarded as he studied Michael. "There's nothing new on Isaacs, I'm assuming?"

"No. But I've got some of our best men looking. The Americans are still asserting that it was his body found in the aftermath of the blast." Michael shifted so that he could meet Gregor's gaze, but the big man was staring off at the horizon, apparently not feeling the same degree of trepidation. "But Joseph is too good at what he does to have let himself be blown up with his own bomb, and he's definitely not the type to martyr himself by committing suicide."

"Agreed," Delafranco said. "But then how do you explain the body?"

"If I had to call it, I'd say it was Stoltz's. After all, he was tasked with taking Isaacs out. And we haven't heard from him since. I'm guessing Isaacs left some kind of trace—something to throw A-Tac off. Something to make them believe it was him in the fire instead. They'd have no way of knowing about Stoltz and so no reason to dig beyond the surface evidence."

"Yes, but A-Tac seems to make a practice of doing exactly what we think they won't."

The words were galling, but true. And Michael had learned a long time ago that the only way to fight fire was with fire. It was time for a showdown. To end things once and for all. "Even if they do figure it out, Stoltz will only be another dead end."

"Maybe," Delafranco said, not sounding convinced, "but if you're right, then Isaacs is still out there somewhere. Which begs the question as to why he hasn't contacted us."

"He's not a fool. Joseph has always been the type to duck for cover at the first sign of trouble." Michael lifted one shoulder in an exaggerated shrug. "I should have anticipated that he'd make a run for it."

"You should have anticipated a lot of things." Delafranco's gaze was hooded, but Michael could still see a flicker of distrust. Maybe Isaacs wasn't the only one he'd underestimated.

"We'll find Isaacs. And when we do, I promise you, he'll cease to be a problem as well."

"And A-Tac?" Delafranco asked. "Thanks to your actions, they're more interested than ever in destroying everything we've worked so hard to build."

Anger flared, and Michael closed his fists, striving to maintain calm. "You leave A-Tac to me."

"Unfortunately, that's not going to be possible, Michael." Delafranco shrugged, the Walther in his hand glinting in the sunlight. "I'm afraid, my friend, that your time with the Consortium has come to an end." Michael Brecht stared down the muzzle of Anthony Delafranco's gun, anger mixing with surprise. He wouldn't have believed his friend capable of such betrayal.

But he recognized the determination in Delafranco's eyes, even as he saw the slight movement of his hand tightening on the trigger. Michael dove for the ground as the quiet garden exploded with gunfire. Pea gravel scraped across the skin on his forearms as he fell, Delafranco's first shot going wild. Behind him, Michael could see his associate Gregor struggling with Delafranco's bodyguard. And as Delafranco tried to readjust the trajectory, Michael scrambled for cover, wishing to hell he had his weapon. This wasn't the way he'd planned for it to end.

More shots rang out, and Michael flinched, then blinked as Delafranco's gun fell from lifeless fingers, his body crumpling forward, blood staining the gravel walkway. Gregor stepped from behind a rose bush, still holding his gun, the bodyguard stretched out beside him.

"You okay, boss?" Gregor asked, kicking away the bodyguard's weapon and bending to check for a pulse. There was no need to check on Delafranco. His blood and brain matter had been sprayed across the roses like macabre graffiti.

"Is the bodyguard dead?" Michael asked, brushing the gravel from his pants, his gaze still on Delafranco.

"Yes." Gregor stood up, holstering his weapon. "We'll need to get the bodies out of here as soon as possible. We don't want any unnecessary questions."

"Agreed. You can call Stephan. He's discreet. And he'll make sure there's nothing for anyone to find."

"Still, you'll have to explain Delafranco's death to the Council."

Michael reached out to pluck a wilted rose from its stem, thinking about the group of men he'd hand-picked to help lead the Consortium. "Eventually. But for now, we'll just let them believe he's disappeared."

"There will be questions."

"That's to be expected. And I trust that you and Stephan will leave a trail of answers. Delafranco would never have dared to try this if he were on his own," Michael admitted, the taste of the words bitter in his mouth. "I need to know who was acting with him. And then we can weed out the rest of the traitors. Once that's done, I'll make sure the others know the real truth. That

I created the Consortium. And that I'm the one in charge. And should anyone else try to interfere, he'll meet the same fate as Delafranco."

"As you wish," Gregor said, nodding his agreement. "But what about A-Tac? Delafranco was right. They are going to continue to be a problem."

"Not to worry. I've got plans for them too. All that remains is to activate the file I embedded in the hard drive I had Kamaal Sahar leave behind at the camp in Afghanistan. And when Avery Solomon and his merry band find it, the wheels will be set in motion. He'll come running, and vengeance will be mine."

Chapter 1

Sunderland College, New York—six months later

All right, chow is served," Avery Solomon said, setting a platter of burgers on the game table in his living room. "First pitch is in five. So fill up your plate and grab a seat."

"Angels are going to kill," Drake Flynn said, sliding two burgers onto his plate along with a healthy serving of potato salad. "Just so you guys are prepared." He settled on the sofa and reached for his beer.

"In your dreams, surfer boy," Nash Brennon laughed, dropping into an armchair as strains of "The Star-Spangled Banner" resounded from the surround-sound system. "Yankees rule."

"Most of the time. But this year your pitching sucks, and we've got Pojuls."

"And not much else," Avery said, settling into a chair. It was good to have some downtime. Of late, it seemed like A-Tac had been spending a hell of a lot of time chasing after ghosts. Most of them sent by their nemesis, a secretive arms cartel known as the Consortium. And despite the fact that they'd managed to win most of the battles, the cost had been high.

Too high, if he had to call it.

But it was what it was, and there was nothing he could do to change the past. Best to focus on the future. And in the moment, the things that made it all worthwhile. Baseball, beer, burgers, and good friends.

"Where's Harrison?" Nash asked, taking a sip from a bottle of Shiner Bock. The beer, a Texas import, was a favorite. And Harrison Blake, recently back from a job consulting with drug enforcement agents about an operation on the Mexican border, had brought Avery a case. "I thought he was supposed to be here."

"He is." Drake nodded. "But he also just got back from almost a month away. And if Hannah is anything like Madeline, let's just say absence really does make the heart…" he trailed off, waggling his eyebrows for effect.

"Jesus, Drake." Nash blew out a disgusted breath. "Do you ever think of anything besides sex?"

"Yeah. Baseball and beer." Drake grinned, lifting his bottle. "The trifecta, of course, being all three at once."

"Good luck with that," Nash snorted, shaking his head.

Avery watched his friends, suddenly feeling too damned old. This business had a way of sucking the life right out of you, particularly when they were dealing with the Consortium. He'd been with American Tactical Intelligence command for more than ten years now.

A black ops division of the CIA, his team was the best of the best. Using Sunderland College as their cover, everyone did double duty as both operatives and professors. And all of them were more than capable of carrying the load.

Nash, a noted historical scholar, was also his second in command. Drake, a renowned archeologist, handled extractions and logistics. Harrison headed the IT department and managed to work magic with computer forensics for the team. Hannah Marshall taught political science and sorted through intel, pulling nuggets of crucial information seemingly from thin air. Tyler Hansen rounded out the team, mixing a love of literature with an uncanny ability to both create and dismantle ordnance. All in all, an extraordinary group of people he was proud to call family.

Avery took another sip of his beer, turning his attention to the TV. The first Angels batter was up with C. C. Sabathia on the mound for the Yankees.

Behind them, the doorbell rang.

"Harrison," Nash said, shooting a sideways glance at Drake as he bit into a burger. "Told you he'd be here."

"It's open," Avery called. C.C. threw a curve ball for strike three.

"Sorry I'm late," Harrison said, something in his expression sending alarm bells jangling. "I sort of got sidetracked." He held up a mangled-looking black box, his eyes telegraphing regret.

"Dude, you're not supposed to be working," Drake protested. "The Angels are playing the Yankees. Where I'm from that's almost sacrosanct."

"Big word, Drake," Nash said, turning to look at Harrison, his eyes narrowing at the sight of the black box in Harrison's hand.

Apparently Avery wasn't the only one to sense that something was up.

Never late for the party, Drake swiveled around, looked first at Harrison, then at Avery, and then back at Harrison again, the game forgotten. "You've pulled something off the drive."

The mangled hard drive had been recovered in an abandoned terrorist encampment in Afghanistan. A-Tac had received intel about the possibility of a Consortium-funded operation, but when they'd arrived, the camp had been abandoned, everything of consequence removed or destroyed.

Except for a notebook that had helped them stop an assassination attempt. And the remains of the hard drive. Avery hadn't doubted for a minute that if there was recoverable information, Harrison would find it. But he'd also been fairly certain that there wouldn't be anything left to find.

Clearly, he'd been wrong.

"I'm sorry," Harrison said. "I know the timing sucks." As if to underscore the sentiment, the solid *swack* of bat meeting ball echoed through the room, but nobody turned to look. Not even Drake. "But you're going to want to see this."

Harrison's gaze locked with Avery's, and suddenly he wasn't all that certain he wanted to know. But there was nothing to be gained in putting off the inevitable. Whatever the Consortium had in store for them next, he was ready.

"Okay then," Avery said, switching the TV off with the remote, then pushing the burgers out of the way as they all gathered around the table, "what have you got?"

"It's a little startling." Harrison paused, clearly searching for the right words. "And kind of personal." His gaze met Avery's. "You might want to hear this on your own."

Avery shook his head, crossing his arms over his chest. "We're all family here. So tell us what you've found."

Harrison hooked the box up to his laptop and hit a key. A woman's face filled the screen. Her dark hair curled around her face, brown eyes glittering with some unshared emotion, her generous mouth giving nothing away.

Avery's heart stopped. His breath stuck in his throat. And he felt as if someone had just kicked him in the gut.

She was dressed in fatigues, standing next to a bearded man

leaning against a table, his hand resting intimately on her knee. "Sweet Jesus," Avery said, the words strangled. "This was on the back-up drive we found in Afghanistan?"

"Yeah." Harrison nodded, his face filled with worry. "I was just as surprised as you are."

"Is that?" Drake said, turning to Nash, who was staring open-mouthed at the photograph.

"Yeah." Nash nodded. "Martin Shrum. Avery's old partner. From before A-Tac days. And Evangeline, Avery's wife. But I thought she was—"

"Dead," Avery finished, emotion cutting through him as he caressed the ring he wore on his little finger. "She is. For almost fourteen years now."

"Yeah, well, Avery, there's more." Harrison clicked the picture so that it zoomed in and then moved it so that they could better see the table behind the two people. "Look at the wall." He enlarged the picture again.

"It's a calendar," Drake said, stating the obvious.

Avery's blood ran cold, his eyes reading the date, his mind trying to process the seemingly impossible.

"Holy shit," Drake continued, his incredulity only adding to the surrealistic horror of the moment. "It's dated December of last year."

* * *

Mekong River, Southeast Asia

"Where's your husband?" Sydney Price asked, laying down her wrench as she scanned the deck of the boat for the missing man.

"He promised he'd be right back." Mary Wilston's voice held a note of apology. "He said there was supposed to be a temple just beyond those trees." She pointed at the thick undergrowth of the Myanmar jungle. "He just wanted to see it."

"And I told you both specifically not to stray beyond the beach." Syd blew out a long breath. She should have known that the idea of seeing the ruins would prove too much for Brian Wilston.

The man had talked about the temples almost nonstop since he'd boarded the boat. If she hadn't been so preoccupied with her own issues, she would have noticed the oil leak before leaving Xieng Kok and they'd be halfway to Tong Phueng by now. But instead, she'd only given the boat a cursory check before setting out with the journalist and his wife. And now, she was clearly being punished for her carelessness.

This particular stretch of the Mekong River was part of Southeast Asia's Golden Triangle. The area where Thailand, Myanmar, and Laos came together. Long known for its opium trade, in recent years, commerce had widened to include other drugs, principally methamphetamine and crystal meth. And like most places known for drug trafficking, there was inherent danger. Both from the drug runners themselves and from those people trying to stop them.

Add to that the fact that the Shan State of Myanmar was still a frontier, its people isolated and impoverished, and seemingly rich tourists made perfect targets. Which was why Syd only ferried people downriver from Xieng Kok to Tong Phueng or carried them upriver to the relative safety of China, always sticking closely to the Laos coastline. There were drug lords in Laos as well, but they were less militant and not as inclined to take hostages.

Unfortunately, when the boat's engine had died, the Laotian side had offered nowhere to pull in, and so she'd been forced to choose a stretch of muddy beach on the Myanmar side instead. She'd instructed both the Wilstons to stay put, but she should have known better.

Tourists. What a pain in the ass.

But these days, they made up the majority of her passengers. People trying to get a feel for the real Southeast Asia, traveling the Mekong from China to Vietnam, usually with stops in Laos, Thailand, and Myanmar along the way.

The Wilstons, arriving in Xieng Kok by bus, had been dismayed to find that the settlement had little to offer in the way of western amenities. Actually if Syd had to call it, she'd say it was Mary who was disappointed. The woman wasn't the roughing-it-in-the-wilderness type. Hell, she didn't belong in this part of the world at all. And her husband was only a little better equipped. Certainly not enough to fend for himself if he ran into hostile locals.

With a sigh, Syd reached for the gun she kept on board. And after checking for ammo, slid it into the waistband of her cotton pants.

"Stay here," she said to Mary, shaking her head when the woman started to argue. "No way are you coming with me. I want you here. Where I know you're safe."

The woman's eyes widened. "You really think there's something to be afraid of?"

"I think it's best not to tempt fate. This is rough country. And it's no place for a foreigner to be wandering around on his own. I'm sure your husband is fine. But I'll feel better when I've got him safely back on the boat."

"But surely you're exaggerating," Mary said.

"I wish I were." Syd shrugged, and motioned Mary into the

boat's cabin. "I'll be back as quickly as I can." She jumped over the side of the boat, wading through the shallow water to the muddy beach. Brian's footprints were still visible, and she followed them into the jungle, pushing aside tree limbs and thorny ferns as she moved carefully forward.

As the jungle closed in around her, the heat descended, thick and heavy, almost smothering. It was the beginning of the rainy season, and water dripped from pretty much everything, adding to the blanketing effect of the oversaturated air. Overhead, high in the canopy, birds chirped as they swooped through the arcing branches, their colors bright against the mottled greens and browns of the trees.

Normally, she loved walking in the jungle. The smell of the damp earth combined with the pungency of the myriad vegetation to form a heady mix that spoke of primordial life. But today her thoughts were limited to her missing passenger. And the potential for trouble. Her fingers grazed the butt of her gun, giving her at least a little reassurance. She wasn't a newcomer to this kind of party, but when a civilian was involved, the game became inherently more dangerous.

The temple, or what was left of it, lay just ahead, and Syd slowed her pace, making sure that she moved silently through the undergrowth. If luck was on her side, she'd simply find Brian taking pictures of the ruins. If not, then she'd best be ready.

As if to underscore the thought, the sound of voices drifted through the undergrowth and Syd drew her weapon, releasing a slow breath as she felt adrenaline flooding through her. It had always been like this—the excitement of confrontation outweighing any fear. Edging forward, she peered between the fronds of a large fern.

The clearing was small. The ruined temple almost completely

engulfed by vegetation. Tree roots curled around the base as vines wound their way up what was left of the stone structure. Brian Wilston was standing with his back to her, gesturing wildly as he tried to explain himself in broken Burmese. The man standing in front of him wore a grim expression and carried a semiautomatic machine gun.

Definitely not a local farmer. He waved the gun toward the jungle behind the fallen temple and then motioned Wilston forward. Although he probably knew Burmese and most likely a smattering of English, the man was speaking Shan, a local dialect that Wilston clearly did not understand.

Syd considered her options. Shooting the man wasn't viable because Wilston was standing directly in the way. And with the man clearly trying to shepherd Wilston into the jungle and possibly back to some sort of encampment, she didn't have time to shift into a better position. If she was going to act, it had to be now. And surprise was her best weapon.

She slid the gun into her front pocket, the loose cotton of her shirt covering its bulk. Better to go in acting the part of boat captain with miscreant passenger. In point of fact, at the moment, that's exactly what she was. Holding her hands out so that the man could see, she walked into the clearing.

"*Kin khao yao ha,*" she said, issuing the standard Shan greeting which translated roughly to "have you eaten." The man lifted his gun a little higher, but his eyes sparked with appreciation.

"I have."

"And was it to your liking?" Syd asked, playing the familiar social game.

The man nodded once, still eyeing her with both suspicion and admiration. Wilston opened his mouth to speak, but Syd shook her head.

"This man is a tourist," Syd continued still speaking in the guttural dialect. "He left my boat without permission. If he has harmed anything here, I apologize. But he is from the West and as such is unfamiliar with your ways."

It was unlikely that Wilston had done anything to the ruined temple, and even more unlikely that the man cared, but it kept the conversation going. As Sydney inched closer, her eyes locked on the man's face, even as her periphery vision registered the exact location of the arm holding the gun.

"You speak Laotian?" the man asked, correctly identifying the lilt in her accent. Although not her actual country of origin, she'd spent much of her childhood there, and because of that, spoke the language like a native.

"I do. I grew up there." No need to tell him the whole truth. Better to let him believe she was, like so many others, a half-breed local. "And I'd like to take my friend back to the boat if that's all right with you."

The man narrowed his eyes, clearly considering his options, then shook his head. "You will both come with me. If your identity checks out, then we will let you go."

It was the word "we" that alarmed her more than anything else. If she allowed him to take them to another location, one with allies, she lost any chance she had for escape. And it was pretty damn clear that the diplomatic route wasn't going to work.

"Fine." She shrugged. "We'll go with you."

Wilston's, wild gaze met hers as the man with the machine gun stepped toward him. Sydney shook her head slightly and then whirled into action, spinning around, her leg slicing through the air, as she simultaneously reached for her weapon. Her foot slammed into the man's arm, sending the machine gun flying.

"Don't move," she said, leveling the gun, "or I'll shoot."

The man eyed her with grudging respect and then lifted his hands in surrender.

Sydney motioned for Wilston to pick up the machine gun.

Once that was accomplished, she told the man to turn around. At first she thought he was going to disobey, but with a grunt of dissatisfaction he did as she asked. She lifted the gun and brought the butt down on the side of his head—hard. The man crumpled to the ground. And satisfied that she'd bought them enough time to get back to the boat, she turned to tell Wilston to go, but he was already thrashing through the jungle, running for the river and the safety of the boat.

Moving backward, gun still drawn, Syd followed, keeping an eye on the surrounding brush for signs of the man's friends. It was tempting to take him out. But the repercussions would cost more than any satisfaction she might have. And besides, life was sacred. Even one as reprehensible as the one in the clearing.

And anyway, there'd be enough explaining to do as it was. Her job was simple. Ferry people up and down the river. Keep her eyes open. And stay out of trouble.

Now, thanks to Brian Wilston and his curiosity, she'd set herself up as a target. The man in the clearing wasn't going to be happy to have been bested, especially by a woman. Which meant that he'd be watching—waiting for an opportunity to get even. Just exactly the kind of attention she didn't want or need.

Stupid-ass tourists.

Chapter 2

Sunderland College, New York

Y̶ou don't have to do this alone," Hannah said, her nose crinkling beneath the bridge of her cat-eyed glasses. "We should be coming with you."

"She's right," Tyler said, crossing her arms as she leaned against the windowsill in Avery's office. Behind her the newly unfurled leaves of an oak tree shimmered in the wind. Avery leaned back in his chair, steepling his fingers, striving for a calm he didn't actually feel.

"I don't need you guys on this one. It's much more important that you tend to business as usual. We've got two ops in play, and we're still trying to figure out who killed Isaacs. I need the two of you, along with the rest of the team, to concentrate on that. My problems are just an added distraction."

"Evangeline could be alive," Hannah said, running a hand through her fuchsia-streaked hair. "I'd hardly call that a distraction."

"Considering the source, I don't think we can believe a word of it." Tyler's frown echoed Avery's own sentiments. "The entire thing feels like a setup."

"The important question being who's pulling the strings," Avery agreed.

"I know you're probably right," Hannah admitted somewhat reluctantly, "but if there's even the slightest chance…"

"Then I have to go," Avery finished with a sigh. "I know. That's why I'm heading to Southeast Asia." The pain of losing his wife wasn't something he relished living through twice, but Hannah was right, he had to be sure.

"And you're sure that Shrum really is in Myanmar?" Tyler asked.

"As much as anyone can be." Hannah shrugged. "The man is so far off the grid, he barely registers. But I've got pretty solid intel that indicates that he's there working as part of the drug trade."

"So why the hell hasn't the CIA come down on him? It isn't as if they don't have dedicated officers monitoring ex-operatives." Tyler frowned.

"He isn't worth the trouble," Hannah said. "Myanmar isn't exactly a user-friendly country. And for the most part, Shrum is only a minor annoyance. Bottom line, there are a hell of a lot bigger fish to try to reel in. My guess is that, between his service record and his low profile, the powers that be have given him a walk."

"Which could be a huge mistake," Avery acknowledged. "Martin was always a wild card. Even when we worked together."

"I assume you were close," Hannah ventured, her concern apparent.

"*Were* being the operative word." He hadn't spoken to Martin since Evangeline died. Hell, for all practical purposes their friendship, such that it was, had ended when Avery had married Evangeline. Although they'd continued working together for just over a year afterward.

"Look, I know there was bad blood between the two of you," Tyler said. "And I know that you don't want to talk about it. So I won't press. But the very fact that you've got a photograph of your supposedly dead wife and Shrum only goes to Hannah's original point. You shouldn't be going into this on your own."

"I'm not," Avery assured her, grateful that she hadn't pushed for more information. He'd known Tyler a long time, and trusted her with his life, but some things were better off left in the past. "The brass have arranged for me to have an escort, an undercover operative running an ongoing investigation into the players inside the Golden Triangle. So our man on the ground already has the infrastructure to move within the region without raising alarms. I definitely don't want Shrum tipped off that I'm coming."

"Well, I wouldn't count on that." Tyler shook her head. "If we're right and the photo was planted for us to find, then the Consortium is up to their necks in this. And that means they'll have a game plan, so it's possible that Shrum will be expecting you."

"Which could mean they're playing you off against one another," Hannah mused. "Unless of course, the photograph is genuine and Evangeline is still alive."

"I assume Harrison still hasn't been able to find a flaw in it?" Avery asked.

"Not yet. But he's still looking and he's called in a friend who's even better with photography than he is. So if it's a fake, we'll figure it out. Maybe you should wait?" Her voice held a hopeful note, but her expression was resigned.

Avery suppressed a smile. "It's not like I can't handle myself on an operation. I've done my share of fieldwork, and for the most part, come out of it unscathed."

"Yes, but we've usually got your back," Tyler said.

"Well, I'll have the help of the guy embedded in Laos."

"But you don't actually know him?"

"No." Avery shook his head, unwilling to share his own misgivings. "But Langley seems to think highly of him. And as I said, the rest of you have more important things to do. Besides, it's not as if I'm falling off the end of the earth."

"Well, it's not exactly an area known for its urbanization and modern technology." Tyler still looked mutinous.

"I think I can help there," Hannah said, breaking in to her first real smile. "Harrison rigged this satellite phone for you. It should be able to connect to us directly no matter where you are." She held out the phone. "So at least you can be in touch."

"Thanks," Avery said. "See, even if you're not there, you'll still have my back."

"I still wish we were going with you," Tyler groused, but her expression too had changed to acceptance. "But since I'm not, I've got a gift too." She reached into a bag slung over her shoulder and produced a stun grenade. "I know you'll be armed to the teeth, but you never know when you might need a little extra fire power. Shock and awe and all that." She paused, awkwardly shifting from one foot to another.

Avery smiled and reached out to give her a hug. "I'll be in and out before you know it."

"Hopefully with good news," Hannah offered.

"Not likely. But I appreciate your optimism." He reached out and squeezed her hand, his gaze encompassing them both. "And I'm glad to know I've got people like you on my side."

Actually, it was the only thing carrying him forward. That and the idea that, by some amazing quirk of fate, his wife was still alive. Of course, even if the miracle did turn out to be true, it only created an even more difficult conundrum. If Evangeline wasn't dead, then why the hell hadn't she tried to contact him?

* * *

Avery stood in the doorway of the bar, rubbing the back of his neck. The flight from New York had been a long and uncomfortable one, the narrow fuselage of the air force cargo plane he'd hitched a ride on too pitched for him to stand upright and too cramped to be truly comfortable even when seated. Add to that the puddle jumper he'd been forced to take from Okinawa, followed by the boat ride from China to Laos, and he was aching, bone tired, and, to be honest, in dire need of a drink.

Truth be told, Avery hadn't expected to find an establishment like this in an outpost like Xieng Kok. Leave it to an Aussie to set up bar in the middle of a jungle. Even if the name painted on the splintered shingle that passed as signage wasn't a dead giveaway—Matilda's—the frayed flag in the window with the Union Jack and the Southern Cross would have identified the proprietor's nationality.

Not that it mattered. Had the place been owned by Martians, he'd still have been damn glad to see it. And even happier to know that his contact had arranged to meet him here. Inside, the crowd was mixed—expats, tourists, and a few locals. A man with a shock of red hair and an unruly beard worked behind the bar. And, typical of a place in the middle of nowhere, Avery's entrance caused little interest. People in this part of the world tended to mind their own business.

Of course that didn't mean they were unaware, just that they weren't overt. The bartender lifted his head for a moment, his gaze assessing, and then turned back to the glass he was filling.

Avery made his way through the crowd and waited for the man to hand off the beer to a patron sitting at the other end of the bar.

"What can I get you, mate?" the redhead asked, his accent confirming Avery's assumption about the barkeep's nationality.

"I'll have a beer," he replied, turning slightly so that he could better see the bar's patrons. It was crowded, people clustered around tables or standing in groups. The sound of laughter and conversation had the comforting ring of like establishments everywhere. And despite the tension of the past few days, Avery felt himself relax, at least a little.

"You're American?" The bartender was back with Avery's beer.

"Yeah. New York." He'd already decided to use his cover as part of Sunderland's faculty, his purported purpose for being in Laos academic research. "I'm here to study the temples."

The man gave him another assessing look and then smiled. "Hell, that's what half the buggers in this country claim to be here for. Funny thing is, I doubt any of them have actually seen one of the damn things. I'm Angus." He held out a beefy hand and Avery shook it, immediately liking the man and his forthright manner.

"Avery." He said, not bothering to lie about his first name but not sharing more than that. His cover would hold if anyone were to check into it, but in a place like this, too much information would only make people suspicious.

"You just in, then?" Angus asked.

"That obvious?"

"Yeah, well, I recognize the signs of someone who's been too long on the river. The Mekong may be beautiful, but she isn't easy." Angus turned away as another patron called for a refill, and Avery took a sip of his beer, the bitter brew cold as it slid down his throat. Movement at the edge of his periphery vision caught his attention, his heart stuttering to a stop as the image of dark curls and liquid brown eyes filled his memory. Evangeline.

He turned, his breath catching in his throat, but then the woman tilted back her head, laughing at something a man at her table had said, the light hitting the smooth blue-black swirl of her long hair and the sun-kissed gold of her skin. Still smiling, she pushed away from the table and, after a final exchange with the man, headed for the back of the bar, disappearing into the crowd.

His stomach clenched as disappointment warred with relief.

"You see someone you know?" Angus asked, appearing again at Avery's elbow, his tone holding nothing more than casual interest.

"No." Avery shook his head, turning his attention back to the barkeep. There was nothing to be gained in letting his imagination get the best of him. "But I am supposed to meeting someone here. A guide. Guy by the name of Sydney Price?"

Angus's craggy face broke into a grin. "Syd's here all right, mate." He shot a look out at the assembled company. "In back at the pool tables." He nodded toward the far corner of the bar. "Just through that archway."

Avery nodded his thanks, then grabbed his beer and made his way through the crowd. The man was still sitting at the table where the woman had been. He'd tipped his chair back so that he could lean against the wall, his eyes on the other patrons in the bar. Watching. Avery recognized the façade even though the man was clearly doing his best to blend in.

Smart move.

In the Golden Triangle, it was probably the safest mode of operation. This was, for all practical purposes, still a frontier. People living life balanced on the edge of a sword. One wrong move and each would be faced with certain disaster. Staying alert in this part of the world was the key to staying alive.

Avery stepped through the archway, his eyes moving again to the woman with the raven hair. She was bending over a table, shifting the pool cue to line up her shot. With one swift move, she drew back the cue and sent the balls flying, three of them spinning into adjacent pockets. Shifting slightly, she lined the cue up again and took a second shot. And then a third and a fourth, effortlessly clearing the table.

The men gathered around her cheered, several letting their gazes linger too long on the curve of her behind as she straightened and shrugged in the direction of a man wearing a faded flak jacket.

"Better luck next time, Edward." The woman's voice was deeper than he'd expected, slightly raspy, and, even more surprising, American.

"Hell," the man said, his accent marking him as British, "You're a Yank. I should have known you'd be a ringer."

The woman laughed and then turned, her emerald gaze both assessing and admiring, the combination disconcerting. It wasn't often that someone caught him off guard. But for one moment, Avery felt as if everyone else in the bar had disappeared. As if it were just the two of them—an electric current stretching tight between them.

Then with a slight twist of her lips, she turned away, taking the shot of whiskey the Brit was offering, downing it with a single swallow.

Avery forced himself to look away, instead concentrating on the rest of the crowd, trying to figure out which of them was the guide the CIA had arranged for him.

"You look lost." It was the woman again, this time her eyes teasing him.

"No," Avery shook his head, answering her smile with his own. "I'm just looking for someone. Sydney Price?"

Her smile widened. "Well, you're in luck, then. Although slightly confused." She stuck out her hand. "I'm Sydney Price. Who the hell are you?"

* * *

Syd's stomach did a double flip as she looked up at the big man standing in front of her. As his hand enveloped hers, she had to remind herself to breathe. When her boss had called to tell her to expect some bigwig from the States, she'd pictured some tight-ass pencil pusher. An overprivileged asshole with too much money and all the right connections.

The image was a far cry from the man standing in front of her. This man—this very *big* man—was clearly not a politico. Every inch of him screamed warrior. The closely cropped hair, the predatory stance, the way he held his head, even the way he shook her hand. This was a man who took prisoners and asked questions later.

His sheer physical presence would make most men cower. But there was also something else, something unexpected. It was there in his eyes. A wisdom at odds with his strength. And an intensity that hinted at some deeper emotion. Some inner power that was far more dangerous than anything he might be capable of physically.

"Avery Solomon," he was saying, his deep voice surrounding her like a warm blanket on a chilly night.

She swallowed, pulling herself into check. She had obviously let her imagination run away with her. Just because the man was better looking than she'd anticipated didn't mean he wasn't still going to be a pain in the ass.

And besides, she wasn't the kind of woman to fall all over herself for a man. It was just the booze talking. She shook her head, and extracted her hand, striving to gain control again. He was the stranger here. And it wasn't as if she'd just fallen off a turnip truck. This was her turf. She'd been undercover along this stretch of the Mekong for more than three years now. And in that time, she'd delivered more credible intel on the Southeast Asian drug trade than any operative before her.

And push come to shove, she was every bit as much a warrior as he was. Strength wasn't only about size. It was about the entire package. And bottom line, she was at the top of her game. Which was totally contradicted by the fact that the man's mere presence had completely gobsmacked her.

Hell, the whiskey had clearly gone right to her head.

Chapter 3

It should be fairly simple." Avery Solomon sat back, his dark eyes giving nothing away. "All I need for you to do is ferry me back upriver and guide me to Shrum's compound. It's my understanding that it's a couple hours' walk from the landing."

Syd sighed, wishing she were thinking more clearly. They'd managed to snag a table in a quiet corner of the bar, but Avery had insisted on getting a bottle of whiskey. Which, on top of the other alcohol she'd consumed, meant that she was feeling no pain.

Normally she didn't drink on the job, but the close call in the jungle the day before had set her nerves on edge, despite the fact that she'd come out on top. People in this part of the world didn't forget easily. And despite the fact that she'd let the man live, she knew she'd made an enemy.

And so she'd allowed herself a moment of freedom, thinking that her encounter with Avery would be brief and about nothing of consequence. Her superiors hadn't bothered to apprise her of his mission. Just the fact that he needed transportation. She'd assumed it was some sort of fact-finding mission or possibly political glad-handing. Instead, he was expecting her to take him into the heart of the Triangle, a part of Myanmar that even the country's own military avoided.

And to make matters worse, he wanted to find Martin Shrum. A minor player, he was nevertheless a crucial one. Because of his interference, several of her team's operations had gone south. Intel lost, kingpins escaping. He might not be trafficking drugs on a major scale, but he was certainly in bed with the people who were. And despite the fact that the suits at Langley had ordered her to turn a blind eye, there was no one she knew who wouldn't like to see him taken out of the equation—permanently.

Of course, given the chance, she'd be the first in line. So maybe this operation would turn out to have value after all.

"Getting to Shrum will be anything but simple." She pushed her half-empty glass back, her mind moving away from the past as she began to consider their options. "He's tucked away in a hill retreat that's hard to reach on a good day. And with the rainy season beginning, the odds of one of those is diminishing by the hour. Add to that the fact that he isn't keen on visitors, and we could have a real problem."

"He'll see me," Avery said, his words brooking no argument. Syd had the feeling that Avery Solomon was the kind of man who usually got what he wanted. No matter what kind of obstacles stood in the way.

"You're friends?" she asked, the idea making her stomach turn. Part of her job was to be able to accurately read people, and she'd lay money on the fact that Avery was someone to be trusted. And Shrum was most decidedly not.

"We were. Once, a long time ago." Avery paused, his gaze clouding with memories, the fingers on his left hand tightening into a fist. Whatever had gone down between the two of them, it hadn't been good.

"So you want to read me in?" She probably shouldn't have asked. She'd been told that the mission was need to know. But she wasn't fond of flying into a situation blind. Especially where Shrum was involved.

He exhaled slowly and tilted his head, clearly considering how much he wanted to share with her. "We were partners back in the day. When he was still with the company. And then we had a falling out. I haven't talked to him since."

"And now?" she prompted, studying his face, listening for something in his voice to identify his true intentions.

"Now, it's possible he has something that belongs to me. And if it turns out to be true, I'm here to take it back."

"Sounds personal." She sat back, completely sober now, her mind turning over the possibilities.

"It is."

"Well, then I'd say you must have some friends in pretty high places for the brass to have allowed you to use operatives on a mission like this."

"Actually, they wouldn't let me use my own team."

"You're still working?" She tried but couldn't keep the surprise from her voice.

"Are you saying I look that old?" His eyebrows lifted, his expression amused.

"No, I just thought—I mean, the way it was presented to me, it seemed like you were someone out of the game."

"And now that you've met me..." He trailed off, the side of his mouth lifting in a crooked grin.

"I'm revising my opinion. Clearly, they should have told me that you were a working operative. Then I would have—"

"What? Killed the fatted calf?" He was openly laughing now, reaching out to pour himself another round. "So they didn't tell you anything?"

"Just that you were coming and that it was need to know. Oh, and that I should do everything in my power to make sure that nothing happens to you."

"And so you assumed I needed a guardian angel."

"I assumed you actually needed my help. If you've got your own unit, then you sure as hell don't need me." She sat back, feeling irritated without really knowing why.

"I just told you, they didn't want me to bring them down here. There were other, more important battles to fight."

"But they didn't object to your coming." It was a statement not a question, but she said it anyway.

"I pulled in a few favors. As you said, I've got some friends in high places."

"And this mission is important to you."

"Vital." A shadow passed across his eyes, and for a moment, his defenses lowered, and she saw a glitter of pain. "And you're wrong about my not needing you. I might not need your protection, but I do need your knowledge. This is your backyard. You know the area and you know the players. And according to my friends at Langley, you're one of the best operatives in the region."

"There are people here who might argue with that." She sat back, reaching for her drink again, suddenly feeling as if she needed the fortification. "So what else did they tell you about me?" Clearly the lack of information disseminated had been limited to her side of the equation.

"That you're something of a loner. And that you don't play well with others." He took a sip of whiskey. "Although based on what

I saw earlier when you were playing pool, I'd say maybe they had it wrong."

"Only their semantics." She shrugged, meeting his gaze head-on. "It's not playing with others that's the problem. It's working with them. I'd just rather do it myself."

His smile widened, his teeth white against his dark skin. "I don't know that I can argue with that. Even after all my years working in tandem with others, some of them the best in the business, I still believe the only person you can truly count on is yourself."

"Not exactly the company mantra."

"Hardly. But then truth be told, we're not really expected to color within the lines, are we?"

She shook her head, answering his smile with one of her own. "No. Although we're definitely supposed to stay in the vicinity." She'd found that out the hard way, her initiative costing far more than any benefit that might have been gained.

"And I take it that hasn't always been the case," he said, uncannily reading her mind. But then she supposed she shouldn't be surprised. Avery Solomon didn't seem the type to miss anything, even the things people thought they kept buried inside.

It should have made her uncomfortable, but for some reason it had the opposite effect, actually making her respect him—something she always found difficult to do. In fact, she could count the number of people she respected on one hand, and most of those she'd known for a hell of a long time. She'd met Avery only a couple of hours ago.

All of which still pointed again to the possibility that she'd lost her mind.

"Yeah, well, I've never been known for doing something just because someone tells me it should be done," she said. "I'd rather be sure it truly needs doing first. I grew up around politi-cos, and believe me, I've learned to recognize bullshit when I see it."

"An admirable trait." Again he surprised her with his reaction. "So how long do you think it will take us to get there?"

"To Shrum?" she asked, pulling her mind away from her wild ramblings and back to the task at hand. "It'll take a day—maybe a day and a half to get up the river."

"Why so long? It took less time than that to get here from China."

"You were coming downriver, and the weather was good. We'll be heading upstream, and if we get caught in a squall, we might have to stop for the night. It's not safe to run a boat once it gets dark."

"Pirates?" he asked, looking interested but not particularly perturbed.

"They can be a problem, yes. Especially since we'll be traveling right through the heart of Wai Yan's territory."

"Wai Yan." Avery said with a frown. "Name is familiar."

"It should be. He's the leader of one of the stronger cartels. Family based. He took over for his father about two years ago. And he's been working diligently since then to expand the busi-ness. Usually by force."

"And he doesn't take kindly to strangers in his waters."

"Exactly. Although he knows me. And there's a sort of grudg-ing truce. As long as he believes I'm not a threat."

"So if he isn't a threat, then who is?"

"The river. Her waters can be treacherous, deep and still one moment, rocky and shallow the next. And with the rains, the problems are only exacerbated. It's hard enough to manage in daylight. But in darkness…only a fool would attempt it."

"Spoken like a true river pilot."

"It's all part of the service." She tipped an imaginary hat at him, realizing that she was coming perilously close to flirting. "Anyway," she said, with a shake of her head, "after we make landfall, it's like I said, it shouldn't take us more than a couple of hours to reach Shrum's compound. Of course that's assuming we don't run into trouble on the way."

"Are you sure you're up for this? I wasn't kidding about no reinforcements. We'll be on our own."

"I'm always on my own." Her smile was a little hollow, and she wondered why the thought gave her pause. She'd never minded before. At least that's what she'd always told herself. It helped her deal. "And as you've already pointed out—that's how I prefer it. Besides, I've got a cover to maintain."

"So when do we leave?"

"No reason to wait," she said, already calculating the things she needed to do. "In fact, with the weather closing in, I'd say better to get on it. I'll have to do a little legwork first—check my intel and lay in supplies—but I'd say we should be able to head out by mid-morning. Which, with luck on our side, should get us to the landing point before dark."

"Sounds like a plan." He lifted his glass. "To adventure."

"And to finding whatever it is that you're looking for," she responded, clinking her glass with his.

Avery swallowed, the motion rippling the muscles in his throat as a shadow chased across his face. Then, with a sigh, he set his glass down, lifting his troubled gaze to hers. "You know my mother always used to tell me that I should be careful what I pray for. Maybe it's best that I not find anything at all."

* * *

At least Sydney had kept her word. She'd managed to arrange everything so that the two of them were off before noon. And as such, they should have been making good time. Unfortunately, the weather hadn't gotten the memo. A few miles upriver from the village, the sun had disappeared and the rain had started. Nothing like Avery had ever seen before, a sheet of water so penetrating nothing could escape it.

"Is it always like this in the rainy season?" he asked, as she fought to steer the boat through the oncoming rush of water that marked the river.

"Worse." She grimaced as she fought the wheel against a swell. "This is nothing by comparison. Not that it matters because we've still got to deal with what we've got."

As if to underscore her words, the fall of rain—already an onslaught—seemed to increase, the sheet of water growing, if possible, even more impenetrable. The boat, typical of those found on the rivers of Laos, was low slung, long and lean, the pilot's cabin, basically a ramshackle wooden lean-to at the bow of the shovel-front power canoe.

A little farther back, a second wooden canopy was meant to serve as protection for passengers, the boat so narrow that if the seats along both sides were occupied, no one could easily pass by. Behind that, about two-thirds along the length of the boat, was the engine box, surrounded by an open hull for cargo that extended from the engine to the stern of the boat.

From a distance, the overall effect was comical, the boat looking as if it were running assbackwards. But in reality, the design worked amazingly well, the captain's upfront position providing the right vantage point for steering past obstacles. Which was exactly what Sydney was doing now.

Ahead a large rock rose out of the gloom, black and slick with rain. To either side, water gushed, churning white and foamy.

"Hang on," she called, her voice whipped away in the wind as she pulled the wheel sharply to the left. "This could get bumpy."

"I think that might be an understatement," Avery observed, reaching out for the railing as the boat rolled suddenly to the starboard side, water splashing onto the deck. Then, just as suddenly, it careened back to the port side, slapping the water with its hull as Sydney struggled to keep the damn thing upright.

The boat lurched again, the motion sending Avery into the roof's support beam, his head crashing into the overhang. This was definitely not a river to be taken lightly. His ears ringing, he found his balance again, grateful to see that Sydney had successfully piloted them around the maelstrom, the water calming a little as the rock faded to a shadow in the river behind them.

"You all right?" she asked, shooting a sideways glance in his direction.

"Fine." He grimaced, rubbing the top of his head. "I don't think this boat was really intended for someone my size."

Sydney smiled, her attention back on the river. "I'll admit most of the people around here barely make it past five feet. But I've got a feeling there aren't that many places in the world that were truly designed for a man your size."

"True enough." He watched as the river rushed past, the trees along the banks bending with the force of the wind. "My mother used to say that if I didn't stop growing, I was going to turn into Paul Bunyan."

"The one with the blue ox, right?" Sydney tilted her head to one side, her braided hair falling over one shoulder.

"Yeah." Avery grinned. "Exactly. And I figured that'd be a pretty good gig. I mean the dude had it going on. At least from the perspective of an eight-year-old. So needless to say, I drank my milk."

"And kept growing."

"To my mother's dismay. Especially when she realized I didn't have the talent to be a basketball player or the desire to play linebacker."

"You look like you could take out a player or two."

"That I can, but I never really saw the point in ramming guys just for the hell of it."

"So you joined the CIA." Her laughter seemed at odds with the relentless fury of the storm, and yet still strangely in sync with it somehow. Sydney Price was definitely in her element.

"Worse," he said, still smiling. "I joined the Marines. Although to be fair, when they ram into somebody, there's usually a damn good reason."

"I'm sure your mother was proud."

"Actually, she wasn't. After basketball didn't pan out, she'd kind of pinned her hopes on more traditional paths. Doctor or lawyer. She wasn't really all that big on the military."

"What about your dad?"

"He was never in the picture. I saw him only once, when I was about five. And it isn't a very good memory."

"I'm sorry," Sydney said, crinkling her nose in apology.

"No worries. We did fine on our own. My mother was strict, but she was always there for me."

"And what about now? How does she feel about your working for Langley?"

Avery sensed there was something more than casual banter to her question. "She never knew. She died before I joined the company. But I suspect she'd have approved even less. My mother was an opinionated woman. And the only thing she was less enamored of than the military was the government. Especially a prejudiced one."

"I can relate to that." Sydney nodded. "On all counts. My mother does know what I do. And she most definitely doesn't approve. She doesn't consider it a fit occupation for an Asian woman."

"But you're an American."

She shook her head. "Try explaining that to my mother. She's from here. Laos. Raised in the Xieng Khouang Province."

"If I'm remembering right, they were hit pretty hard during the Vietnam War."

"Yeah, mostly by U.S. troops. I think it must have been really bad. My mother was only a little girl, but it definitely made an impression. And not a good one. Which is why my mother share's your mother's opinion of the U.S. military and by association the CIA."

"But she married a U.S. citizen," Avery prompted, curious now.

"She did. And my dad is as American as they come. Part Cherokee, actually. Born in the panhandle of Texas. They met when he was living in Laos, teaching English. It was love at first sight. In fact, there's really only ever been room in their lives for the two of them. I was more like an afterthought."

"Were you born in Laos?"

"Nope. Amarillo. But I spent some of my summers here. With *ma tao.*"

"Your grandmother."

"You speak Lao." She looked impressed, so much so that Avery found himself wishing that he actually could speak the language.

"No. Just a smattering. I've worked a couple of operations in this part of the world. So I've picked up a few words here and there. But I doubt I could hold a conversation."

"Well, even a little is better than nothing." She smiled. "People here will respect you for making the effort. Most foreigners don't."

"So is that why you got posted here? Your fluency with the language and, I'm assuming, the culture?"

"I imagine it's why I got the job. But as far as the posting itself, I asked for it. Don't get me wrong, I love Texas and I love America. But there's a part of me that's just more comfortable here."

"And, as far as Langley is concerned, it's definitely an asset to have someone here who can pass as a native."

"Actually, I've never tried. I just play the mixed-race card. There are a lot of people here who fit that profile. Not really fitting into one culture or the other." She shrugged. "I've felt that way most of my life. Both when I was living with my parents and when I was living here with my grandmother. After a while it starts to define you."

"I certainly can understand that. I think that's where my mother was coming from all those years ago when she was fighting my career with the Marines. She wanted more than anything for me to be respected. And at least from her perspective, that wasn't going to happen there."

"Well, if my intel on you and your unit is even half right, then I'd say you've more than proved her wrong."

"Don't believe everything you hear." It was his turn to smile.

"No chance of that. Cynicism is programmed into my DNA. On both sides." She turned the wheel to avoid a swell. "Anyway, the thing our mothers don't understand is that it's different now from when they were growing up."

"In some ways, definitely. But in others..." He trailed off, surprised at the serious turn of their conversation.

"It is what it is, I guess." She shrugged. "Anyway, add to all of that the fact that I'm a spook, and it isn't really all that surprising that my mother disapproves of my choices. She's all about the marriage-and-kids thing. Women in their proper places."

"And your father?" Avery asked.

"I don't know that he really cares what I do. I mean, he cares about me. And he wants me to be happy and safe and all that. But he's really too involved with his own life to give too much thought to mine."

"Is he still teaching?"

Sydney was silent for a moment, watching the river and the rain as she chewed on her bottom lip. "No. He works for the government. He's in the diplomatic core."

"I see." Avery frowned. "That must have been difficult for your mother."

"She's just happy to be with him. One of the benefits of true love, I guess."

"You say that like you don't buy it."

"I don't think anyone should subjugate themselves to someone else. No matter what emotion is involved."

"You weren't kidding about the cynicism." He studied her profile for a minute, noting the stubborn jut of her chin. "It's possible that what you see as subjugation is just commitment. Putting another person first isn't always a bad thing."

"Have you ever been in love like that?"

"Yes," he said. "Once." The word hung between them for a moment. It was the first time he'd felt uncomfortable around her, and he immediately regretted it, but he wasn't ready to talk about Evangeline. "So where's your father stationed?" he asked.

"At the moment, Vienna." Again she paused, and he was afraid she was going to ask him about his wife, but instead she sighed. "He's the ambassador there."

Avery frowned. "I thought Marshall Walker was the Austrian ambassador?"

"He is," Syd acknowledged, with a wry twist of her lips. "And he's also my father."

"But your name is Price."

"It's actually my paternal grandmother's name. I started using it just after college, when I was first looking for a job. I didn't want people to think I was trading on my father's status. If you've heard of him, then you know he's had a rather successful career."

An understatement. Marshall Walker was a mover and shaker. The top of the list when it came to D.C. headliners. There had even been talk of his running for president.

"It's just easier to divorce myself from all of that," she continued. "Especially since I've been working with the CIA. There's potential for real danger if the wrong people were to make the connection."

"I'm surprised actually that they let you do fieldwork—even with the name change."

"Well, I've always worked covert operations for one thing. Which means my cover is pretty damn tight. And my background is buried really deep. And it doesn't hurt that no one out here really gives a damn about the ins and outs of American politics. Besides, I'm good at what I do. Anyway, you're one to talk—*Professor* Solomon."

"Dean of students actually—and I'm pretty damn good at doing that. But you're right, of course. Langley has made an art form out of creating covers. I was just surprised. I actually know your father, professionally at least."

"Then you must run in some pretty high-level circles." She turned with a frown, her gaze assessing now. "My father isn't the shake-hands-with-the-plebeians type."

"We served on a task force together once. And I've run into him from time to time in Washington over the years. Anyway, the point is, I've always been impressed."

"He's a good man. Just a little myopic when it comes to certain things." Again Sydney shrugged, but Avery had the feeling that there was more to it than that, but he didn't know her well enough to push for more. And besides, he had more important things to deal with—like finding Shrum and, potentially, Evangeline.

Chapter 4

Syd slipped a sideways glance at Avery, then turned her attention back to the river. She wasn't sure why she'd told him the truth about her father. It wasn't something she usually discussed. But he'd asked her point blank and there was just something about the man that demanded truth. She wondered again just exactly who Avery Solomon really was. Clearly there was more to the man than just his job with A-Tac. Which in and of itself was pretty damn impressive.

When she'd pressed her contacts for information, she'd been surprised with the range and accomplishments of the team Avery had assembled. They'd single-handedly managed to thwart a number of potentially deadly terrorist attacks, including an assassination attempt on one of the Middle East's rising diplomatic stars.

A-Tac was definitely one of Langley's most elite units. And Avery had headed the team since its inception. Which made it all that much more puzzling that he'd come here on his own without their backing. She'd have understood if the op was off the books, but her orders had come from the top—the very top. And yet, here he was, hunting Shrum on his own.

Not that she was complaining. The opportunity to work with someone of Avery's caliber was a definite turn-on. And there was always the chance, if she handled it right, that she could segue this gig into a permanent placement with A-Tac. She'd hadn't lied when she'd told Avery that she preferred going solo. But that didn't mean she didn't want to advance her career, and one way to do that was to make sure you were surrounded by the best of the best.

It was one of the lessons her father had drilled into her at an early age. Always play tennis with people better than you. Much, much better.

And if her intel was right, Avery Solomon was as good as they got.

"Any chance this is going to let up?" Avery asked, breaking into her cascading thoughts.

She looked up at the swollen sky and shook her head. "Probably not. It looks like it's socked in for the rest of the day. Or what's left of it." She glanced down at her watch, surprised to see how late it had gotten.

"So have you got somewhere we can put in for the night?" Avery asked, his gaze moving to the river banks and the palm trees whipping wildly in the wind.

"I was hoping we'd make it as far as the cut off to Shrum's. But it doesn't look like that's going to happen. Better to just find a place to hunker down and ride out the storm. Then we can try again in the morning. There's a place a couple miles up the river from here, belongs to a friend of mine." *Belonged*. She contained a shudder. She hadn't been to Tim's place since he died. Too many memories. Still, this wasn't the time to let emotion stand in the way. "It's nothing fancy but it should be dry."

"Beats sleeping in the rain," Avery said, with a shrug.

"Sorry this hasn't exactly been a luxury cruise." She forced a smile, pushing her thoughts firmly to the present.

"I knew what I was signing on for," he assured her. "You're the one who's being asked to take an unnecessary risk. This isn't exactly a sanctioned op."

She turned to him in surprise. "But my orders came straight from Langley. I was told to give you carte blanche. No way is this mission off-book."

"I didn't say it was," he said, his liquid brown gaze meeting hers. "I said it was unsanctioned."

"It means the same thing." She studied his face, trying to figure out what it was she was missing.

"Actually, it doesn't. If you go off-book, and believe me, I've been there and done that, you're completely on your own. If you're unsanctioned, you're acting within the protection of the company."

"Until it all goes south," she said. "At that point, the results are exactly the same. Langley hangs you out to dry."

"Well, there are differences. But I'll grant you the outcome is pretty much identical."

"And finding Shrum is important enough for you to hang your career on it?"

"Yeah, for me it is. But that's not necessarily the case for you. I'd just assumed they'd read you in enough to know what the risks were. But since they haven't, and since your career is only just starting, I'll totally understand if you want to opt out."

"And what? Leave you on the river bank with a map?" She shook her head with a laugh. "I've no doubt that you're good at what you do. And I'm sure you're more than adept at handling dangerous situations. But sanctioned or not, your safety has been charged to me. And I'm not one to step down from a challenge.

Besides, so far the only real danger we've faced has been the river."

"Famous last words," Avery said, the thought clearly meant as a joke, but when he stilled suddenly, his brows drawing together as he turned to face the river behind them, she felt a shiver of worry trace its way up her spine.

"You seeing something?" She asked, shifting so that she could better follow his line of sight.

"I don't know. Between the dusk and the rain, it's hard to be sure of anything really. Add the sharp bends and twisting trees and I'm probably jumping at shadows."

"But—" she prompted.

"But I thought I saw another boat out there. Smaller. And definitely faster. If I'm right, it's still pretty far behind us."

"Yeah, but if it's a speedboat, it'll catch up really quick."

"You think it's Wai Yan?"

"Hard to say, these guys don't exactly display their colors. But it's a strong possibility."

"You said you had a truce. You think we should be worried?" he asked.

"I think out here, we'd be foolish not to at least pay attention." To underscore the fact, she opened a small footlocker sitting at the base of the wheelhouse, pulling out a pair of field glasses. "See if you can spot anything. And in the meantime, I'll see what I can do to fortify our position." She bent again and pulled out a rifle and then a handgun, sliding the gun into the space at the small of her back, then checking the chamber of the rifle.

"You see anything?"

"Roger that," Avery acknowledged, handing her the glasses. "Seven o'clock, port side."

Syd took the glasses and gave Avery the rifle, which he slung over his shoulder, then she turned so that she could see the water behind them. At first, there was nothing but the heavy mist from the rain, but then a shadow detached itself from the far bank, the outline of the boat becoming more defined. Definitely a speedboat.

"Looks like it's closing fast." She lowered the glasses, turning her attention back to the river in front of her, yanking the wheel to avoid a boulder jutting up out of the water. "Damned if we do, damned if we don't," she said, more to herself than anything, but Avery heard her.

He rechecked the rifle and then tested its weight against his shoulder. "Glad to know my guide is prepared."

"There's more ammo in the locker." She nodded, still concentrating on the rush of water ahead. "And a couple of smaller guns as well. I keep them out of sight most of the time. But as I said, no sense in taking chances. It's nasty weather, and it's almost dark. I'd say anyone on the river is suspect."

"Including us," Avery said, pulling a Walther PPK from a side pocket in his duffel. Like Syd, he slid it into the waistband of his pants.

"Yeah, well, there aren't really any truly good guys, are there?" She'd meant the words to be teasing, but somehow they'd come out a little stronger than she'd intended.

"I don't know about that," Avery said. "I just think one has to choose one's heroes carefully."

"So you really believe in heroes?"

"I work with them every day."

The words were spoken with understated conviction, and she found them oddly comforting. Although she wasn't really sure she believed them. People always had their own reasons for doing things. It was just the way humans were built. Self-preservation was hard-wired.

"We can discuss the finer points of that argument later." She shrugged. "But right now, I suggest we concentrate on our friends out there. Could be Wai Yan, could be from another cartel, but either way I'd say the odds are pretty strong that they're not on our side. The only question remaining—are their intentions malignant or benign?"

"Judging from the gun mounted on the front of the boat," Avery said, looking through the field glasses again, "I'd say the former. Any chance we can outrun them?"

"Not unless you know something about this crate that I don't. She's damn near indestructible, but she was never meant to move quickly. I can try to outmaneuver them, but there's no way I can beat them in a full-out sprint."

"All right then, we gear up for the possibility of a battle."

She glanced back at the boat behind them, steadily closing the distance. "With a twelve-inch on the bow, I'd say we're a little outgunned."

"I've been in worse situations." Avery's smile was contagious. "What else have you got on board in the way of munitions?"

"Nothing that's going to compete with that." She nodded toward the speedboat. "Just the guns I mentioned and a stick or two of leftover dynamite. I transported some of the stuff downriver last month, near the Thai border, for an outfit building a casino on the Myanmar side. It's over there." She nodded to the port side of the wheelhouse.

"Could have potential," he said, frowning as he clearly turned over the possibilities. "So, the way I see it, we've got two options. We can try to take them out. If I had the chance, I could try to shoot at their fuel tank."

"You'd have to be a hell of shot," she said. "Even in perfect weather. But in this?" She nodded at the torrential downpour.

"It's not an impossible notion," Avery mused. "Although it would mean we'd have to pull well within range."

"Which doesn't seem like the best idea considering they've got the big gun. And I'm assuming we've got the same problem with the dynamite."

"Yeah, I'm afraid we'd be sitting ducks. Which might be worth it, if it was a sure thing. But as you pointed out, there are other mitigating factors that stand in the way of certain success."

"So you said there were two options. What's the second choice?"

"We make ourselves a nonissue."

"So what? You think we should surrender?" She narrowed her eyes and straightened into every inch of her five-foot-three frame. "The last thing we need to do is give them more of an upper hand than they already have."

"I wasn't suggesting that at all." He held up a hand in apology. "It would be too dangerous. Even with our covers, there's always the chance they'll figure out who we really are. Or worse, they could already know. It's possible Shrum found out I'm coming and isn't all that keen on a reunion."

"Or maybe it's someone who has an ax to grind with me," Syd said, thinking of the man she'd hit in the jungle. "This isn't exactly a world where people play nice. And I've made my share of enemies."

"So we're agreed—either way we can't take the risk."

"Okay, so then if we're not going to try and fight, and we're not going to surrender, what do you propose?"

"You're not going to like it."

"If it means we get out of this alive, then believe me, I'm all for it," she said, pushing the throttle to maximum power, the engine coughing and sputtering in response, the speedboat only seconds behind them now. "And I'd say sooner's better than later."

"All right. So if we can't blow up their boat, I think we should blow up ours."

"Are you out of your mind?" The words came out of their own accord, and for a minute, she forgot who it was she was talking to.

For a moment, his jaw tightened, and she had a glimpse of the steel that he kept hidden behind his quiet façade. This was not a man to be trifled with. Still, it was her damned boat and her damned life, and she wasn't going to give in to some half-baked idea just because the idea came from Avery-fucking-Solomon.

She squared off, anger making her reckless. But before she could say anything, his expression softened, his mouth breaking into a disarming smile. A fire sparked inside, somewhere just south of her belly, and she was surprised at the intensity. Damn the man. "If you think—" she started, but he cut her off with a finger to her lips, and she struggled to breathe, her senses threatening full-out revolt. What the hell?

"Hang on. Give me a chance to explain," he said, shooting a look at the boat, which was now clearly visible behind them, even in the dark gloom of the rain. "I think it's our best chance." He waited, his dark-eyed gaze moving back to hers, his finger still pressed against her lips.

She nodded, and he stepped back.

"I know you love this boat," he began, "but destroying it is our best chance out of this mess. If they think they've hit us, and that we were taken out with the boat, then our problems are solved. So all I've got to do is rig the dynamite to blow the engine and we should be set."

"And how do you propose we avoid being actually blown to bits?"

"Easy. I'll rig it on delay, and we'll slip into the water before it blows. With any luck at all, they'll think we're dead, and their problem is solved."

"And we do what? Swim to shore and steal another boat?"

"Seems like a fair plan. You said your friend has a place up the river a bit. Does he have a boat?"

She nodded, turning the idea over in her head. She hated the idea of losing her boat. In a weird way, it had become her home. But at the end of the day, it was just a vessel. And Avery was right, it might be their only option. As if to echo the thought, the speedboat behind them opened fire, a hail of bullets strafing the aft floor and railing.

"If we're going to make this work, we've got to move fast." He could have pulled rank. Ordered her to obey. But instead, he was asking, even as gunfire echoed around them.

"What do you want me to do?" she asked.

"Rig the throttle so that it'll keep moving forward. And then put everything that might be of value in my bag. It's waterproof. So it'll protect even the weapons. Then, as soon as you've got that done, head over to the starboard gate and slip into the water. I'll be right behind you."

The boat fired again, the bullets closer this time, one whizzing just past her ear. "Go," she said, already turning to grab a cable with a d-ring to tie open the throttle.

He nodded, reaching down to grab the dynamite and a clip of ammo. "With any luck, I can rig the gunpowder as a fuse." She had to admit there was a certain genius to the plan. With another quick nod, he sprinted toward the back of the boat and the engine box, keeping low to avoid the gunfire.

With the throttle open and the boat moving forward on its own, Syd grabbed the weapons and the ammo and stuffed them into Avery's neoprene bag. She added some rations and a couple bottles of water, then slung it over her shoulder, grabbing her own go-bag as she moved toward the starboard side of the boat. Bullets were hailing all around her now, and she used the boat's benches and canopy to shield her.

Despite her growing concern, she resisted the urge to check on Avery. He could handle himself. What he needed now was for her to do her part. With a last spurt she darted across the open space between the passenger bench and the wooden gate that opened from the side of the boat to allow for disembarking.

Her fingers trembled in the cold rain as she fumbled to open it, but finally, the sodden wood yielded to her pressure and swung back, the rain-swollen river rushing by just below her feet. Peering through the quickly deepening shadows, she could just make out the river bank. The trick would be to fight across the current to the calmer water just beyond the boat.

The hull next to the opening splintered as another hail of bullets slammed into the boat. She glanced back to try to find Avery, but the rain obscured her vision, and so she turned back to the water. It was now or never. And as another volley of bullets sprayed across the deck behind her, she looped the bags around her shoulders and slid into the water, praying that Avery would be following behind her.

The current was stronger than she'd expected, the water pulling her downward. She sputtered, fighting her way back to the surface. And then, kicking hard, she began to swim toward the shore, the rush of the water drowning out the sound of the gunfire behind her.

Then suddenly the night sky lit up like a Christmas tree, sparks shooting high into the air as a plume of flame and smoke billowed upward. She could actually feel the heat from the explosion washing across the surface of the water.

Safe in the slower current, out of the sightline of the speedboat, she frantically scanned the surface of the river, looking for Avery. Heart pounding, she treaded water, the empty river making a mockery of her search. If anything happened to him, there would be hell to pay.

And yet, even as she had the thought, she knew her worry stemmed from something more. She might not believe in heroes, but if there were such a thing, she was pretty damn certain that Avery Solomon would make the cut. And the idea that he might not have made it was more than she wanted to contemplate.

She pushed a clump of wet hair out of her face, watching as the speedboat slowly circled what was left of her boat. As it passed the bow, it seemed to hesitate for a moment, and then she heard the engines kick into high gear as the little boat sped off into the night, leaving behind the quiet of the river and the eerie glow of burning wreckage.

Avery's plan had worked.

Now if only she could find him.

Beside her something surfaced in a spray of water, the big man appearing like freaking Poseidon. Hell, he even had the trident—if a rifle counted.

"Where the hell have you been?" she asked, embarrassed by the rough emotion in her voice. But she'd already lost one friend and she didn't think she could stand losing another.

"Watching the show. I wanted to be sure they bought into the fiction. If not…" He trailed off, lifting the rifle.

"Well, I'm glad you're all right," she said, working to make her voice sound more impassive. "I'd have hated to have to explain losing you to Langley."

"There'd have definitely been some paperwork," he said, laughter coloring his voice. And even though she couldn't see his eyes, she could feel the warmth of his gaze. "But it's all good. The ruse worked. And the hostiles have most definitely bugged out."

"And if they did know who we are, then I'm guessing word of our demise is going to spread pretty damn quickly. Power is the name of the game out here. And he who destroys the enemy curries respect." She shivered, still watching the burning remnants of her vessel.

Avery reached out to take the bags, still strapped around her body. She rolled her shoulders in relief, her muscles beginning to shake as the rush of adrenaline and relief faded.

"We need to get you out of the river," Avery said. "Somewhere dry. Will you be able to find your friend's place on foot?"

"Shouldn't be a problem," she said, her teeth chattering with the effort. Damn it. The last thing she needed was to fall apart now. The battle had been won. And she hadn't even done the hard part.

"All right then, I'll follow your lead."

Syd took a last look at the remnants of her boat, then sucked in a deep breath and set out for the shore, the little voice in her head chiding that Avery Solomon wasn't the kind of man to follow anyone. Ever.

Chapter 5

Sydney's friend's shack was more of a lean-to than anything else. A wooden frame dug back into the side of a hill, with thatching for walls and a rough-hewn platform serving as a floor. Palm trees arched overhead, the patter of the rain on their leaves adding a tympanic score to the otherwise still night.

A battered pot-bellied stove stood in the far corner, and somehow, Sydney had managed to coax the water-laden wood stacked on the porch into catching fire. Although the night wasn't particularly chilly, the heat felt good nevertheless, their dunk in the river leaving them both wet and uncomfortable.

Two lanterns hung from the rafters, providing flickering light, and a third sat on the table near the stove. Sydney had rigged a clothesline of sorts using an old piece of rope strung between the stove's exhaust pipe and the window frame, their dripping clothes framing the window like some kind of bedraggled curtains.

Avery wore a pair of dry cotton pants from his go-bag. And Sydney wore his T-shirt, the damn thing practically swallowing her, hanging well below her knees—yet somehow, the effect was all the more alluring.

He knew he shouldn't be thinking like that. Hell, he shouldn't even be looking, but the truth was that she was a beautiful woman, and he'd have had to be dead not to notice the fact. And besides, he'd always had a thing for strong women. And Sydney Price was definitely that.

He rubbed a finger across the smooth gold of Evangeline's wedding band. The cool metal reminding him of why he was here. And why he couldn't let his mind go down that particular path. He wasn't free to think like that. Hell, for all he knew, he'd been living a lie for the past fourteen years. It was just so damn hard to get his head around it all. If Evangeline was actually alive…he tightened his fingers, slamming his fist against the rickety table.

"You okay?" Sydney asked, turning around, her green eyes filled with concern.

"Yeah, sorry. Just thinking about your boat. I'm sorry I had to destroy it."

Sydney shrugged as she set a plate of food in front of him. "You said it yourself. It was our best option." She smiled, the gesture not quite reaching her eyes as she put a second plate on the table and sat down across from him.

"This looks good," Avery said, focusing on the food, feeling somehow as if he'd left his feelings bare for her to see. And the idea didn't sit all that comfortably.

"Well, I didn't have much to work with." She handed him a bottle of water. "Some mangoes, some beans, and some rice. It's not exactly haute cuisine. More like local comfort food."

"From where I'm sitting," he said around a forkful of food, "it doesn't get any better. In fact, it's exactly what we needed after our little river adventure."

"You think they really bought into the show?" Her gaze

darted to the window and then back to the table again, her expression still showing concern.

"Yeah. If they hadn't believed we were dead, they'd have stayed to search the river. Although it won't hurt to keep watch tonight. Just to be sure."

"At least we're on the Laos side. It should be safer over here." She shrugged as she dug into her plate of rice and beans.

"For what it's worth," Avery said, the strength of his regret surprising him, "I really am sorry I got you into this."

"Part of the job. And hopefully, in the end, it'll all be worth it." She tilted her head, studying him, waiting.

His first instinct was to duck the unasked question. But then he thought about her boat and the explosion, and just how easily she'd taken it all in stride. He figured he owed her an answer. A real one.

He reached for the water bottle, taking a long swallow, and then set it back on the table. "A few months back, we were sent on a mission to Afghanistan."

She nodded without comment, sitting back, arms crossed. He liked the fact that she didn't pepper him with questions, giving him time to tell the story in his own way.

"There was intel that suggested a village in the mountains was really a terrorist encampment. We executed a raid, but they'd evidently gotten word we were coming. Except for a lone sniper, the place was deserted. We scoured their headquarters and managed to come up with some pretty damning intelligence. Enough to help us thwart an attack on Manhattan."

"You're talking about the bombings in the city. And the assassination attempt." They were statements, not questions. Sydney had apparently done her homework.

"Yes. Anyway, in addition to the other stuff we found, there was also a hard drive. Partially destroyed. Virtually unreadable. But my tech guru, Harrison Blake, is the kind that won't give up on a puzzle, and so he kept at it. And finally, last week, he managed to pull something off the damn thing."

"Something that led you here—to find Shrum." Again, she was giving him an out. A way to keep his own council, and again he realized that in doing so, she'd actually convinced him she deserved the whole truth.

"Harrison found a picture of my wife."

Sydney's gaze shot to his empty ring finger and then to the gold band on his little finger, her eyebrows moving together in confusion.

"My wife died fourteen years ago," he said, cutting to the chase. "Or at least that's what I believed. Until I saw the picture." He paused to take another sip of water, ordering his thoughts, then reached down to the bag at his feet, producing a copy of the image. "This is what he found."

Sydney picked up the photograph, tilting it so that she could see it better in the lantern light. "That's Shrum." She frowned down at the picture, her eyes moving across it. "And I take it that's your wife?"

Avery nodded. "Evangeline."

"And you think this is real? I mean, these days it's pretty damn easy to fake this sort of thing."

"Agreed. But Harrison hasn't been able to prove that it was manipulated. So at least some part of me has accepted that it's real. It's just that…"

"She doesn't look like a captive," Sydney said, finishing his thought. "And if she's not being held against her will, then…" It was her turn to leave the sentence unfinished. "God, I don't know what I'd do if I were in your shoes."

"You'd come out here and try to find the truth."

"Yeah, I guess I would." She was still studying the photo. "Does she look older?"

"I don't know," Avery said, tilting back his head on a sigh. "I've stared at the thing so much now, I don't even know what I'm seeing anymore. I mean, I know it's her, but the picture is grainy and her face is in shadow, so I can't really tell if she's aged."

"Well, even if it did look that way, that kind of thing can be manipulated too. But the real question here is why someone in Afghanistan, conceivably a terrorist, would have the picture in the first place."

Again he was struck by her consideration. She wasn't asking about his marriage. Or even about Evangeline's death. She was focusing on the photo and the mission. Of course, that would have been part of her training. At Langley, subtlety was always the key. Still, he couldn't shake the sense that it was something more. That she was trying to spare him the pain of reliving all the details.

"That's the question I've been asking since we found the damn thing. My team thinks there's a possibility the whole thing was a setup. A way to lure us in."

"You think it's Shrum?" The idea clearly surprised her.

"I don't think we can rule it out. But there's nothing in the intel we have on him to indicate he's in bed with anyone in the Middle East. And nothing that ties him directly to terrorists."

"Beyond aiding and abetting the drug trade," Sydney added. "Although, believe me, if Shrum wants something badly enough, he'll go to any lengths to obtain it. But that said, I'd have to agree with you. I don't see Shrum being connected to something that big. Although clearly, somebody has got a bead on him. If they're close enough to get pictures."

Avery nodded his agreement. "There's a group we've been

tracking for a few years now. They call themselves the Consortium. We don't really know that much about them. But we think they're a highly organized network of arms dealers playing for the highest of stakes. We believe they were behind the assassination attempt in Manhattan and the bombings. As well as a couple other attempts to attack the city. We also linked them to the terrorist camp in Afghanistan."

"So you think they wanted you to find the hard drive."

"Maybe. Or maybe there's something bigger at play here and we really uncovered it. But either way, I'd bet my life that the Consortium is involved. They've got a hard-on for A-Tac. We've been a pretty big thorn in their side for a while now."

"And so you think they planted the photo to get you out here."

"It wouldn't surprise me if they were trying to keep us distracted. When they've got something big on the burner, they tend to try to use smoke screens to pull us off the scent."

"Well, I'd certainly say that this counts as a distraction. Which is obviously why Langley didn't want your team to come."

"Exactly. But even if it is meant as a distraction, that doesn't mean there's not something legitimate going on. For all I know, they're using the photo to try to tip me off to something Shrum is doing."

"Distract you while helping you find your wife?"

"When you put it like that, it sounds crazy. Hell, I don't know." He ran a hand across the top of his head, helplessness cascading through him. It wasn't an emotion he was comfortable with. "Truth is, my gut tells me this is just some kind of macabre joke. A way to throw me off my game. But then I start thinking what if it's not—what if, for whatever reason, the tip is real?"

"Then like I said before, you have to find out. It's as simple as that." Sydney was quiet for a moment, staring down at her hands, and then she lifted her eyes, her gaze colliding with his. "It was Evangeline you were talking about earlier. When we were talking about true love."

"It was."

"You loved her very much." Her voice was soft, almost wistful, and the tone surprised him.

"I did. Evangeline was an amazing woman. In the beginning, I couldn't even believe she was interested in me. In fact, I don't think she was at first. Shrum was the one with all the charm. And he was the one who first approached her. We were in a bar. In Marseilles. She was drinking with a couple of friends. And Shrum bought them a round. We all got drunk and traded war stories…"

"And the rest is history."

"No. It wasn't that easy, believe me. But perseverance won the day. I wore her down and, in the end, I prevailed. Truth was, I don't think I ever really realized how lucky I was. Or how easily it could all be ripped away. If I had, I would have handled things differently."

"I think most people would say the same. We're just not programmed to be introspective like that. Life is best lived in the moment. And besides, it's hard to believe that tomorrow is anything but inevitable. Especially when we're young."

"Well, considering you're not exactly over the hill yet, I'm going to take that as incredibly insightful."

"I'm not as young as I look," she smiled, but there was a hint of sadness. "Or maybe it's just that I feel a lot older than I am."

"This job will do that to you." Avery nodded, surprised at the camaraderie he felt in the moment.

"So what happened, to Evangeline, I mean?" she asked, her eyes telegraphing apology. "I'm assuming you never saw a body or there wouldn't be any question that the photograph was faked."

"You're right. There was nothing left to see." His finger moved automatically to the smooth gold of Evangeline's ring. "She was killed in a roadside bombing in Iraq. The vehicle, and everyone inside it, was destroyed."

"But you're sure she was there?"

"Yeah." Pain stabbed through him, the memory bitter. "There were witnesses. People who knew she was in the Humvee. But it was chaotic. An ambush. So anything was possible."

"But they found her ring." Her eyes moved again to the gold band, her voice hesitant, as if she knew that he was trying to tip-toe through the memory.

"In the rubble. Yes." He lifted his gaze, pulling free from the past. "When I got it, I still didn't accept it as truth. But after digging around, interviewing folks on the ground, I finally had to accept that Evangeline was gone."

"So if you were working with Shrum, you were already CIA?"

"Yeah, but still wet behind the ears."

"And Evangeline? You said you first met in a bar?"

He nodded, smiling despite the pain of the memory, seeing her dark eyes and curling hair. "She was a reporter. And the meeting was totally by accident, but it turned out she was working on an investigation that crossed with an op we were running. So we agreed to pool our resources."

"Shrum too?"

Avery's mood darkened as he thought about the man he'd once considered his friend. "We were like the Three Musketeers in those days. Until Evangeline and I became an item."

"I take it Shrum didn't approve?"

"More like he wished it were him instead of me. Evangeline drew men like flies to honey. And Martin was no exception. Hell, I wasn't any different. I just happened to take home the prize."

"And that didn't sit well with Shrum?"

"He dealt with it. But things were never the same between us after that."

"So how did Evangeline end up in Iraq? I know you were stationed in Eastern Europe."

"She pulled some strings to get embedded with the troops. It was before the days when that kind of thing was routine. I didn't even know she'd gone until they notified me about her death."

"So you were married, but you weren't living together?" Sydney was frowning now, clearly trying to put the pieces together.

"No, we shared an apartment. When we could. But we both had active careers, to say the least, and we were often pulled in opposite directions. It was just part of who we were." He sighed. "Evangeline was really good at what she did. She was a reporter in her soul. Born to be in the middle of the action, telling people the cold, hard truth. I admired that about her. But it made her reckless."

"And you didn't want her to take those kinds of risks."

"No. It's perverse, I know, when you consider what I do for a living. But it's different when it's someone you love. Anyway, we had a real fight about the possibility of her going into Iraq. Things were really unsettled there at the time. And she wanted me to set her up. Use my military contacts to get her a ticket to the front lines." He closed his eyes for a moment, then opened them.

"We had a huge fight. I refused to help her. I even refused to let her go—as Neanderthal as that sounds. And before we could resolve the issue, I got called away on a mission. I figured we'd work it out after I got back. After she'd had the chance to cool off."

"Only she went in anyway."

"And never came back." He nodded, the pain rocketing

through him, as strong now as it had been fourteen years ago. "And the last things I said to her were so damned awful."

"Yes, but she knew you loved her."

He looked down at the picture. "Maybe. Or maybe she figured she'd chosen the wrong guy."

"I'm not following," Sydney's eyes darkened with confusion.

"Shrum was the one who got her the clearance. He's the one who sent her into Iraq. Hell, I thought he was the one who got her killed. All these years, I've blamed him for her death. But what if I got it wrong? What if Evangeline simply decided she didn't love me anymore? What if she decided she wanted to be with Martin?"

"You can't believe that. You said yourself that what the two of you had was special."

"What the hell do I know?" He pushed the picture away, his gaze meeting hers. "Maybe I've just been lying to myself. I mean, if this photo is to be believed, then my wife is alive and living with Martin Shrum. So tell me, what else am I supposed to think?"

Chapter 6

Koln, Germany

I just got solid confirmation from our people on the ground," Gregor said, striding into the office. "Avery Solomon is in Laos. And he's on the move."

Michael pushed aside the papers he'd been reading, sitting back to watch his number two, a spark of anticipation igniting in his gut. "You're sure?"

"Yes. He took off from Xieng Kok early this morning, Laos time. And he appears to be headed for Myanmar and Shrum. Although thanks to some local militants, he almost didn't make it."

"What happened?" Michael frowned. It wasn't as if he'd lament Solomon's loss, but he'd put a hell of a lot of time and energy into creating the opportunity to destroy the man himself. First emotionally, then professionally, and now, considering the man's propensity to meddle, it was time to take him out physically as well.

"One of Wai Yan's patrol on the river had him outmanned and outgunned. But Solomon managed to turn the tables. He blew up his own boat, theoretically killing himself in the process.

Wai Yan's men apparently bought into the ruse. They circled the wreckage once and then left it to burn in the river."

"And you're certain that Avery escaped?"

"Positive. Our man has been following him since he left China. And he says he saw them crawling out of the river fifteen minutes after the other boat was gone."

"Them?"

"Yes. It seems he's with another operative."

"Someone from his team?" Michael questioned, his mind already trying to figure out which of the A-Tac stooges might also be caught in his trap.

"No. According to our intel, Solomon arrived on his own. No sign of anyone else from the team. But he immediately contacted a local CIA plant."

"And where are they now?"

"Holed up in a shanty on the Laos side of the river. Do you want our man to take them out? It should be easy enough."

"Never underestimate your opponent, Gregor. Especially when it's Avery Solomon. Best to leave him alone for now. Besides, I want him to have time to dwell on his wife's potential infidelity." Michael reached out to adjust the photograph sitting on his desk, his heart twisting as he stared at the laughing face portrayed there. "Let it eat at him for a while."

"If that's what you wish." The other man's voice held a trace of doubt.

"It's what I order. I'll not have you questioning my decisions." He gaze collided with Gregor's. "If you aren't up to all of this—"

"You know that I am," Gregor said, cutting him off. "It's just that your quest for vengeance has cost the organization. And there are those that are questioning your leadership. Delafranco's attempt to take you out is proof of that."

"His attempt ended in failure. That's the important thing to remember. And that's what the others will take from it. And although it may seem as though my personal goal has overridden my professional one, it's really quite the contrary—one is simply feeding into the other."

"And I support that. I just want you to be careful," Gregory chided.

"I am always careful, my friend. Always."

"Then take him out now. While it's easy."

"But you forget, there's still the matter of Shrum. He's become quite a thorn in our sides of late. He never lets anything go. Just like Avery Solomon. In their own way, they both present a threat to the Consortium. Funny how everything always comes full circle. And now we have the opportunity to take them out in one fell swoop. So we stick to the original plan." He paused, letting the words sink in, then leaned forward. "Tell me about this other operative."

"She's been in the region for a couple of years now. According to our intel, her cover involves running a ferry service on the river. Solomon was posing as a professor who'd hired her to show him some of the local temples."

"So the boat that they blew up was hers."

"Seems to be the case," Gregor agreed with a nod.

"Could be the attack on the river was about her then. Not that it really matters as long as they think they're both dead. Do we have a name?" In truth, he really didn't give a damn, but it wouldn't hurt to understand the details. If things didn't go as planned, the girl might be useful somehow. Solomon had always had a weakness when it came to women.

"Sydney Price," Gregor said. "I tried to dig up more information, but whoever she is, her cover is solid and her past is buried pretty deep. I don't even know if that's her real name."

Michael sat back with a smile, remembering a conversation in a sunny vineyard just outside of Vienna. "Oh, it's real all right."

"You know her?" Gregor's bushy eyebrows rose in surprise.

"Not personally, no. But I know her father." He paused for a moment—waiting for effect. "In fact, you know him too. Marshall Walker."

"The Austrian ambassador?" If possible, Gregor looked even more surprised. "Could be a fortuitous coincidence."

"I don't believe in coincidence," Michael responded. "We've been trying for months to figure out a way to pull Walker into the fold. Or at least tap into his resources. But the man is squeaky clean and doesn't seem inclined to play traitor. But maybe we can use his daughter to force his hand. He's a proud man—agreeing to side with us won't be an easy decision. But he's fond of his daughter, and I can't imagine he'd abandon her for the sake of principle."

"But if things go as planned, the girl will die along with Solomon. There's no time to use her for leverage."

"It's not too late. We still have options," Michael mused. "Our men have been trained in extraction even under the most difficult of circumstances. I don't see why we can't liberate Ms. Price at the same time we obliterate Solomon and Shrum."

* * *

"I don't buy it." Syd crossed her arms over her chest, studying Avery, wondering why it was that she wanted so very much to erase the pain from his face. Maybe because he'd saved her out there on the river, or maybe it was something more—something she didn't want to think about. Especially not now, in light of all that he'd just revealed. "It's overkill. If Evangeline was truly that angry, she'd have confronted you with it. Not created some elaborate scam to make you believe she was dead. It just doesn't make sense."

"And yet the photo exists." He ran a hand across the top of his head, a gesture she was beginning to recognize as a sign that he was distraught. Not that she blamed him.

The two of them had moved out onto the ramshackle porch of the shack, both of them armed as they talked, at the same time scouring the shadows of the jungle for signs that they weren't alone.

"But why would Evangeline go to such elaborate efforts just because you had a fight?"

He was standing inches away. Close enough that she could feel his body heat. But she resisted the urge to reach out to him, knowing that it was important to maintain her distance.

"I mean, you're right," she continued, "forbidding her to go was a bit Cro-Magnon, but the extreme reaction to that would be divorce, not creating some kind of elaborate scheme to disappear with your ex-partner. It's just not a plausible scenario. Unless..." she paused, biting her lip, hating to put voice to the words.

"Unless there's more to the story?" he finished for her. "No. There's nothing I haven't told you. At least as far as I know, that is."

"Before Iraq, was there ever anything that made you believe something was going on between Evangeline and Shrum?" She stared out at the night, not willing to face him with the question, but she could feel him tensing next to her, his hand tightening around the porch railing.

"No. And believe me I've been over and over it in my head. Martin, I'm sure, would have liked for me to believe that there was something. But I never saw anything to make me believe my wife was interested in anyone but me."

"But you said Shrum was charming." The idea was repugnant, but somewhere in the recesses of her brain, she could see that it once might have been true.

"He was. Is…for all I know," Avery replied. "But Evangeline wasn't the kind of woman to play games. Once she'd made her choice—that was it."

"Which only underscores the fact that her staging her death just to avoid you doesn't make any sense."

"So maybe there was something else. Maybe I just didn't want to see it."

This time she reached out to cover his hand, turning so that their gazes met in the darkness. "I haven't known you very long, Avery. But I'd bet my life on the fact that there isn't much you miss. And if you honestly believe there was nothing going on, then I don't believe it either."

The heat from his hand radiated through her.

"Thank you." The words were simple, and Sydney suppressed a shiver. A woman like Evangeline would have been a fool to throw someone like Avery aside. Especially for a man like Shrum. Which is why the idea was preposterous.

She pulled her hand free with a shrug. "I'm only stating the obvious."

"So you think she's dead."

"I think there's no way to be certain until we check it out. But I don't believe for a moment that she is living there of her own free will. If she's alive, then there's got to be another explanation."

"Well, for the life of me, I don't know what it could be."

"Maybe Shrum has something on her. Or maybe he's been

threatening you. If I loved someone that much I'd go to any extreme to protect them."

"Shrum was competitive. And he most definitely wanted Evangeline, but I don't see him using blackmail to force a woman to stay with him."

"What if he's lied to her? What if she thinks you're dead?"

"Then he's more despicable than I already believed." He clenched a fist, his jaw tightening in anger. "If that bastard has done anything to hurt her…"

"We don't know that, Avery. All of this is just speculation based on a photograph you found on a suspicious hard drive."

"The Consortium is jerking me around. Hell, this is exactly what they wanted me to do. Question myself. And my memories of my wife."

"You said they've done this before. Played on the team's emotions to keep you distracted."

"Yeah. Harrison, the computer guy I was telling you about. He lost his sister to a serial killer. And they fucked him over royally in an effort to keep us chasing our tails. Made him believe the killer was back."

"Jesus. Have there been others?"

"In a manner of speaking. One of my team was turned. And another member was framed in the process—he was murdered. Damn near tore us all apart."

"So when you say that this Consortium is gunning for A-Tac, you're not kidding."

"They've tried to destroy us. First from the inside, and then with distractions in an effort to make us look inept. And finally threatening team member's lives. Take all of that and add in the terrorist threats, and it's been a real ride. But so far, we've always managed to come out on top. Except that there always seems to be another move. These guys, whoever they are, they don't give up."

"Case in point." Sydney nodded, chewing her bottom lip, wondering what it would be like to be part of a team like that. She'd been on her own so long she'd forgotten what it was like to depend on other people. The truth was that, when the opportunity presented itself, she'd pushed it away, and then realized she'd made a mistake—only it had been too late to fix it.

They stood for a moment in silence, watching the palm trees bending in the wind. It was a complicated situation. And Sydney knew herself well enough to know that she was on dangerous ground. But she was also a professional. Which meant her personal feelings had no relevance. She had a job to do. And Avery needed her help. It was as simple as that.

"So you and Shrum parted ways? After the explosion in Iraq, I mean."

"Yes." He nodded. "As I said, when I found out he was the one who'd arranged for her to be in Iraq in the first place, I was furious. And he was already angry with me."

"For marrying her," Sydney said, checking her gun, needing to do something with her hands, her heart twisting at the obvious pain on his face. Avery Solomon was a man who felt things deeply.

"And for winning. Everything has always been a contest with Martin."

"With most men, I think. Especially when it comes to women."

"You really do have a problem with relationships." He tilted his head, studying her, and she nervously holstered the gun, feeling suddenly exposed.

"Let's just say I haven't got the best the track record. But I'm afraid that's par for the course when you've lived your life in the shadow of a *great love*."

"You're talking about your parents."

"Yes." She forced a smile. "It's almost impossible to measure up. But it doesn't matter, I'm much happier here doing what I do."

"Now you sound like Evangeline."

"Well, I'll take that as a compliment. Because no matter how much you want to blame yourself for what happened, it was never your choice to make. If she wanted to go, then she was going to find a way. Whether you helped her or not."

"I know intellectually that you're right. It's just harder to accept that emotionally."

"Emotions are fickle. They tell you what you want to hear. Good or bad. If you ask me, we'd be better off without them."

"I think it's our emotions that make us human," Avery said, his tone resolute. "And it's our humanity that sets us apart." He shrugged, with a crooked grin. "Who knew I was such a philosopher?"

"I think maybe you're wiser than you know." Sydney kept her voice light, following his lead.

The time for deep conversation was clearly at an end. Which suited her just fine. There was something about Avery Solomon that made her want to bare her soul. And at least in her experience, that never lead to anything good.

Chapter 7

The water was choppy. Remnants from yesterday's storm, palm fronds and dead branches, rushed past the boat as Sydney and Avery worked their way upriver. As promised, Sydney's friend had indeed had a boat. But unfortunately, the little craft wasn't much more than a battered dinghy with a rusty, old outboard motor.

They'd left with the dawn, what there was of it, the sky heavy with threatening rain. The river was narrower here, trees arcing out over the water on both sides, creating an undulating canopy of green and brown.

"How much farther?" Avery asked, scanning the jungle on the Myanmar side.

"Just around the next bend," Sydney replied from her perch in the back of the boat as she steered the little craft through the racing water. "Why? Is there a problem?" Her voice tightened with concern, her gaze sweeping across the river.

"Nothing we can't handle," Avery said with a shrug. "It's just that we seem to be taking on water. I guess your friend isn't big on upkeep when it comes to his boat." He scooped water into an empty pail, dumping it over the side to emphasize his point.

A shadow slid across Sydney's face, her eyes flashing for a moment with pain. "My friend"—she paused, clearly reaching for words—"is dead. Which makes it a little hard for him to maintain his belongings."

"Sydney"—Avery's big voice had dropped to a whisper—"I'm sorry. I had no idea."

"It's okay." She held up a hand, clearly not comfortable with the discussion. "You had no way of knowing. I just...I couldn't...it's just that Tim loved that stupid shack. And the boat. He said in our business you always had to have a safe house. Even in a godforsaken place like Laos. His words, not mine."

"He was with the Company?" Avery hadn't been briefed about a colleague dying. And he wondered how Langley could have missed something so important.

"British intelligence actually. He was here working on a drug case. Trying to track a supply line. I helped him when I could. And over time we became friends." They'd been a lot more than that if Avery was reading her right, but this wasn't the time to press for personal details.

"So what happened?" he asked, his gut telling him that her answer mattered.

"Someone threatened me." She blew out a breath, her gaze still on the river. "And Tim took it upon himself to put an end to it. Only he walked into an ambush and wound up dead instead." Her hand tightened on the tiller. "Martin Shrum killed him. But it was my fault."

"Martin? What the hell are you talking about?"

"He was trying to strong-arm me into using my boat to ferry his merchandise. He had no idea who I really was. And I told

Tim that I could handle it. But he wasn't exactly a sit-on-the-sidelines kind of guy. Look, it's a long story, but the bottom line is that Shrum's men were waiting for him. I think maybe that was the plan all along. He played me to maneuver Tim."

"Shrum was at the end of the supply line Tim had been following."

She shot him a look of surprise.

"I told you I'm a quick study." He gave her a tight smile while clenching his fist at the thought that Shrum had caused her this kind of pain. "But even if he did use you to get to your friend, that doesn't make it your fault."

"The hell it doesn't. I should have figured it out. But instead, I let my guard down, and everything got all screwed up. I let emotion get in the way, and Tim paid the ultimate price for it."

"He was a grown man, Sydney. He made his own choices. And besides, if Shrum was after Tim, he'd have found a way to get him. Whether you were part of the equation or not."

"Maybe…I don't know. The truth is, I've played it over so many times in my mind, I don't know what to think anymore." She lifted her gaze to meet his. "Except that I hate Shrum."

"Sydney, believe me, I understand what it is to hate the man. But if your leading me to Martin is going to be a problem for you, I need to know it now."

She lifted her chin, her shoulders straightening. "No. I'm fine. I promise you. I know I should have told you from the outset. But it's hard for me to talk about."

"Understandable," he said. "But right now, my operation has to come first. If there's a chance that my wife is still alive…"

"We have to do whatever it takes to get her back." She nodded. "But once we know…" She trailed off, her expression resolute. "All I'm saying is that when things are clear, if there's the slightest provocation, I can't promise you that I won't take advantage of the opening and do what needs to be done."

"I can live with that," he said, meaning every word and knowing in his heart, that given the chance, he'd probably be tempted to do the same. "But for either of us to have a chance of facing the man, we need to get the hell out of this boat." He gestured to the water, which was now almost five inches deep.

"So keep bailing," she said, forcing a smile, even though the pain was still reflected in her eyes.

Again, he marveled at her strength. In one day, he'd blown up her boat and dropped the bombshell about his real reason for being in country. And now he was asking her to put aside her own personal agenda to take up his. And without any need for cajoling, she'd agreed, taking it all in stride.

He'd surprised himself last night—sharing details he hadn't even shared with his closest friends. Maybe it was the intimacy of the situation. The narrow escape, the shack in the woods, the shared clothing. Or maybe it was something more. He didn't have the time to analyze it. And quite honestly, he wasn't sure he wanted to examine it any further anyway. His life was complicated enough as it was.

Still, as he baled water and watched her maneuver the little boat around an outcrop of jagged rocks, he was cognizant enough to realize that what had started as admiration was moving in an entirely different direction now.

Not that he was free to do anything about it.

He blew out a long breath, tilting his head back and closing his eyes. He hadn't had a hell of a lot of sleep last night. Half of it had been spent on watch. And the other, tossing and turning in the hammock that had served as a bed, his mind playing and replaying a tape of his last night with Evangeline.

Sydney was right. There was nothing he could have done to stop Evangeline from going to Iraq. But he could have handled it so much better. Let her know how important she was to him. How much he needed her. Tried somehow to make her understand that, in going, she wasn't just risking her life—she was risking his.

But instead he'd acted like an idiot. Not realizing that the words he threw at her so carelessly would be the last.

"We're here." Sydney's voice cut through his thoughts.

Avery dropped the bucket and swung out of the boat into the ankle-high water, Sydney following suit. Together they pulled the leaky craft onto the shore and behind a tumble of rock, the dinghy almost completely hidden in the vegetation. He didn't like the odds of it being their method of escape, but it never hurt to be prepared. Which meant it was also probably time to touch base with his team. He liked the idea of someone besides just him and Sydney knowing the entire scope of the situation.

He reached into the go-bag and retrieved the sat phone Hannah had given him.

"E.T. phone home?" Sydney quipped as she checked out the rest of their remaining equipment.

"Something like that. I figure it never hurts to have backup even if it is halfway across the globe." He turned the phone on, a green light indicating there was battery power. But the usual accompanying staccato burst of static was missing. He switched to a second channel and then a third with the same results.

"I gather it isn't working?" Sydney asked, a line forming between her brows as she frowned.

"No. It's live but I'm not getting any reception. Not even any static."

"Could be it was damaged when we went overboard." She sat

back on her heels, tilting her head to one side. "Or it might be the jungle. The river is narrow here, and the canopy is heavy. Not to mention the hills." She nodded at the rock-strewn slopes rising from the jungle behind them.

"I think it's more likely a malfunction," Avery said, trying the damn phone again. "We've used them in scenarios far worse than this. Do you have a radio?"

"I had one. On the boat." She shrugged. "But we kind of obliterated it."

"So I guess that means no backup," Avery said, tossing the phone back into the bag.

"I'll take the odds." Sydney grinned as she pushed to her feet, throwing the second bag over her shoulder and tucking a gun into the waistband of her pants. "We've done all right so far."

"That we have," Avery agreed, surprised to find that he really wasn't worried. He'd have liked to have Hannah and Harrison in his back pocket, but in truth, there was only so much they could do from this far away. And besides, they were probably better off out of this. If things did go south, the Company was going to wash its hands of the whole damn thing. Best there not be anything to blow back onto his team. "So which way?"

"Just through there." Sydney pointed. "Past the big tree. You can see the faint markings of the trail."

He nodded, although he wasn't actually sure that he could. But then that's why he needed her along for the ride. For a moment, he felt a surge of guilt. This wasn't her battle. But then again, she had her own bone to pick with Shrum. Which made her both the perfect partner and a potential liability.

"You're worrying that I'm going to get in your way, aren't you?" she asked, almost as if she'd been privy to his thoughts. "I told you I wouldn't be a problem. At least not until we're sure what's what."

"I know," Avery said, slipping the go-bag over his shoulders. "I just don't want us walking into anything without considering all the options."

"I get it. But I promise, I've told you everything you need to know." The shadow was back, and he knew that there was more to the story, but he was fairly certain it involved the true nature of her relationship with the British intel officer—not Shrum. Sydney held her emotions close to the vest, a fact that Avery respected—hell, understood—and he saw no need to push her for personal information she wasn't ready to share.

If it became pertinent, he had no doubt she'd come clean.

And if it didn't, then it wasn't really any of his business. Although he was surprised to realize that a part of him felt differently, almost as if there were, in fact, something between them. He shook his head, shooting her a smile as he cleared away his wandering thoughts. "Let's do this."

Sydney nodded, her gaze moving toward the slight opening in the trees. "I'll take the lead. We should be alone in there for a good while, but keep your eyes open."

"Roger that," Avery said, patting the comfortable bulk of the rifle slung across one shoulder as they moved into the dense undergrowth.

The air immediately grew hotter and more humid, the heavy stillness surrounding them as they moved forward. The faint light from gaps in the canopy barely made it to the jungle floor, which meant they were moving through relative darkness, mud sucking at their feet and insects buzzing around their heads.

The quiet was occasionally broken by the call of birds high over their heads or a slight rustle as they disturbed some kind of animal along the way. There was no sign at all of human habitation. And only the slight rise in the pathway indicated they were still moving in the direction of the rocky hills where Shrum had his compound. "Are you sure you know where you're going?" he asked, more for something to say than because he really doubted her abilities.

"It's a mix of instinct and familiarity," she replied, without breaking stride. "That and the fact that I've got a compass." She shot him a smile over her shoulder as she lifted her watch to underscore the words. "Shrum is basically due north of here. We just need to keep walking until the trees start to break a little. Once we're in the hills, the jungle should open up a bit, and we'll begin to see more rocks. From there, it'll just be a matter of following the coordinates I programmed into the GPS on my watch."

"Sounds like a plan. Do you think there will be a reception committee?"

"Count on it," she said, pulling out a knife to cut away a large vine blocking their way. "The entrance to Shrum's compound is accessed via a narrow passageway through the rocks cresting the hills surrounding it. Sort of his personal version of the hole-in-the-wall."

"A fan of Westerns or Western history?" he asked.

"History." She shot him another grin, obviously pleased that he'd gotten the reference. "My dad is a huge fan of all things involving the Wild West. The hole-in-the-wall gang and their infamous hideout landing somewhere close to the top of the list. Anyway, Shrum's place is every bit as inaccessible as the Wyoming pass was."

"So how do you propose we get in without risking someone trying to stop us?"

"Two choices," she said as they clambered across a fallen tree trunk. "We can go in arms raised, and hope Shrum's sentimental about the old days. Or we can try an alternative route through a cavern just to the south of the entrance. It's narrow, but there's a passage through. I imagine it'll be guarded, but less heavily so."

"Well, I wouldn't count on Martin's rolling out the red carpet. For me or for you." He'd meant it as a quip, but somehow it came out sounding more accusatory than he'd intended.

She whipped around. "I told you I was sorry."

"I know." He lifted his hands in supplication. "I was trying to make a joke."

She studied him for a moment, eyes still flashing, and then nodded with a little laugh. "I guess maybe I need to chill out a little. It's just that the last time I was here there wasn't a happy ending."

"So we'll go through the cavern and hopefully find Shrum before he has the chance to counter our attack. Unless he's truly hiding something monumental, he's got no reason to kill me without at least having a conversation."

"Famous last words." She moved forward again, pushing aside the arcing leaves from fledgling palms.

"Don't I know it," Avery said, wondering, not for the first time, if he was on a fool's errand. But the only way to know for certain was to confront Shrum. It was what it was. Foolish or otherwise. "So when Martin tried to recruit you—I take it didn't go well."

She was silent for a moment as she fought with another vine and then pushed it aside. "At first it was fairly routine. His people just kept approaching me with various offers. And I kept turning them down. I thought it actually might have been a good way for me to gain inside information into the drug trade, but the powers-that-be felt otherwise."

"But he wasn't interested in taking no for an answer."

"Got it in one. In fact, he was damn persistent. Or at least his people were. Shrum rarely ventures out of his fortress. Better to rule from a distance and let others do the dirty work. Anyway, first with offers of money and protection. And then with threats."

Avery felt himself tense at the thought that Shrum might have hurt her. "Physically?"

"Not specifically, no. But they sabotaged my boat a couple of times. And they cornered me in the bar one night."

Avery tightened a fist even though there was no one to confront, but held his tongue. Sydney was more than capable of taking care of herself, and besides they were talking about the past.

"It wasn't much fun, but suffice it to say I managed to hold my own."

"Did you report it to your superiors?"

"In a manner of speaking."

"Meaning no."

"I told them there was pressure. But not the specifics. I've worked very hard to be accepted as a female operative in this part of the world. And part of that has meant handling things on my own. Crying out for help would have just given them an excuse to send my ass home."

He wanted to tell her she was wrong, but he knew it wouldn't be the truth. "Had I been in your shoes, I probably would have done the same."

"The salient point is that you couldn't have been in my shoes." Again she shot him a smile. "Anyway, I thought I'd handled things. But then one night, I caught two of Shrum's henchmen on my boat. Only this time they weren't trying to disable it. They were seeding it with drugs. Stolen ones."

"Trying to get you in trouble with one of the other cartels."

"Wai Yen's actually. Had I been caught, it would have meant a death sentence. But fortunately, I was able to take care of things."

"Meaning what?" he asked, not sure he wanted to know the answer.

"I didn't have a choice. I took them out. And then Tim helped me dispose of the bodies and the drugs."

"And then he decided to take matters into his own hands." They moved carefully across a tumble of stones, monkeys shrieking over their heads.

"Yeah. Pretty much," she agreed. "He already had a bead on Shrum and the authorization to deal with the situation as deemed necessary. If he'd told me what he was going to do…" She trailed off, hacking viciously at a sapling at the edge of scree.

"You probably couldn't have stopped him. It's in our nature to protect, I'm afraid. Especially when someone we love is threatened."

She stopped, the broken tree falling to the side, her words almost a whisper. "I didn't ask for him to love me."

"I'm afraid that's not the way it works." He wished there were something more that he could say, but it wasn't anything he could fix. He knew from personal experience that Sydney had to deal with her demons on her own. "Anyway, all I'm saying is that even if he'd told you, you couldn't have stopped him."

"I know, but I can't help playing devil's advocate. Basically, what if–ing myself to death."

"Been there and done that. So I understand how hard it is to turn it off. But I also know that there's nothing to be gained in second guessing our decisions. Especially the ones that can't be altered."

"Like forbidding your wife to go into Iraq?" She was moving again, her tone taking any sting out of her words. Besides, everyone had their crosses to bear.

"Exactly. And I wasn't implying that I'd managed to do it. Just that it was important to try. So what happened? With Tim and Shrum, I mean."

"According to his people, he had credible intel that Shrum was going to be on his own at the compound. And that Tim would be able to get in and out, using the caverns, without any problem. But apparently it was all a ruse. They were waiting for him. He didn't stand a chance."

"I'm sorry."

"I'm not the one who needs the sympathy."

"Tim is dead, whatever you believe or don't believe about an afterlife, he's past caring about what happened."

"Makes me envious." She blew out a breath and then shook her head. "Look, I know it's all in the past. And I know that taking out Shrum isn't going to bring Tim back. Or change the way things were between us. So you really don't have to worry about me going rogue or anything."

"I wasn't worried. I just care." And the minute the words were out of his mouth, he knew that, as preposterous as it seemed, she had come to mean a great deal to him in a very short period of time.

She turned to face him, emotions chasing across her face that he wasn't about to try to name. "I actually believe you're serious."

"Of course I am." For a minute they stood, the implication of their exchange not lost on either of them.

Then with the tiniest of smiles, Sydney turned back to the jungle. "It's not much farther," she said, the formality of her tone sending a clear message that heart-to-heart time was over. Which was just as well, since there was no fucking way he was in a position to answer the question reflected in her eyes. Not while there was a chance that Evangeline was still alive.

Chapter 8

Syd fought against the ripple of joy Avery's words had instigated. Despite the heat of the moment, she knew better. He was married. And even if it turned out that Evangeline was truly dead, the man still wore her ring, for heaven's sake.

And besides, if she truly cared about the man, and God help her she did, then she had to hope that they found Evangeline alive. It was an unselfish thought, and she tried to talk herself into believing that all she wanted was Avery's happiness. But in truth, she wasn't a saint. Far from it. And so her brain insisted on trotting out other images, other possibilities.

She sighed, pushing aside her errant thoughts. There was nothing to be gained in imagining a future that could never be. Even if he were available, there were a million reasons why it wouldn't work. She was just caught up in the magnetism of the man.

Behind her, Avery swore as he fought to free himself from a thorny vine, and Syd swallowed a smile. Maybe he was just a mortal after all.

"You okay?" she called over her shoulder.

"Fine," he groused. "Just some minor scratches. Damn thing didn't want to let go. So we're close?"

"Almost there," she replied, looking down at the GPS reading on her watch. "The trees are already starting to thin a bit. There should be a lichen-covered rock next to a tree coming up on our right."

"So you were here?" Avery asked. "After Tim was killed?"

"Not in the cavern itself. But I was part of the team that found his body. Or what was left of it." She shuddered at the memory, the image branded forever in her brain. "They strung him up. As a warning, I suppose. Fortunately, they assure me, he was already dead. But still it wasn't pretty."

"I wish there were something I could say that would make the memory easier, but there isn't. Was there any effort at retaliation?"

"No. My cover was still in place. And everyone felt it was better to keep it that way. It allowed for our continued efforts to monitor the drug trafficking in the area." She tried to keep her voice matter-of-fact, but it was difficult, her mind swimming with memories.

"But you didn't agree with the decision."

"On a practical level, sure, I got it. Above all else, maintain the operation. But from a personal level, I felt like Tim deserved better."

"So how long ago was this?" Avery asked, as they slowed to move around another fallen tree.

"Almost two months. So I guess it's still pretty fresh."

"And has Shrum hassled you any further?"

"Not that I can prove. But someone messed with the motor of my boat a few days ago. Nothing I couldn't fix, but it did force me to land on the Myanmar side."

"But nothing happened?" They moved past the last of the tree and its foliage, correcting their course accordingly.

"Actually, yeah, I had a run-in with a local, but he wasn't really interested in trading information." She consulted her watch again and cut sharply to the right. "One of my tourists got itchy feet while I was trying to repair the boat. He headed for an abandoned temple nearby, and by the time I caught up with him, the local guy had him at gunpoint."

"Kidnapping attempt."

"Considering that the tourist was still alive, I'm thinking yes. Although it never occurred to me that he could have been looking for me. He did try to take both of us away with him."

"*Try* being the operative word, I'm assuming." She could hear the smile in Avery's voice.

"Yeah. I managed to get the gun away from him and then knock him out. We ran for the boat and thankfully made a clean getaway."

"And if I'm guessing right, he's most likely out there somewhere nursing a hell of a headache and waiting for payback."

"Probably."

"And if he does work for Shrum—"

"Then that makes me even more of a liability," she finished for him.

"Not if I have anything to do with it," Avery said, his voice sounding gruff with anger. "But we'll have to play it carefully if we want your cover to stay intact."

"To hell with that. The only thing that matters right now is getting you safely to Shrum and to the truth." Sydney pulled up short as the trees cleared slightly. In the open space a yellow-and-green-covered boulder sat at the foot of a large teak tree.

"Is this it?" Avery asked, coming to stand beside her.

She nodded, her eyes welling with tears as her memory trotted out the vision of Tim hanging from the branches. Avery reached out, his big hand covering her shoulder, his warmth seeping into her, helping her to pull away from the pain.

"I'm sorry about your friend."

"I know. Me, too. He was a good guy." Guilt cut through her, and she wished again that things could have been different.

"It's a risk we all take." Avery's voice carried a note of hard truth, but he kept his hand on her shoulder, his touch somehow making the words more palatable.

"Yeah, but it doesn't make it any easier to lose someone."

"No. I don't think anything can prepare us for that. But what we can do is honor them in the best way we can—by doing our jobs well."

"Which means finding Shrum and taking him down."

"Metaphorically speaking." He smiled at her, the warmth easing her pain. "But in order to do that we're going to need to locate this cavern of yours."

Fifteen minutes later, they were no closer to finding it. Despite Sydney's coordinates, the rock-studded hillside had stubbornly refused to produce anything at all that looked like an opening.

"It's got to be here somewhere," she said, pushing her sweat-damp hair out of her face. "We're just not seeing it."

"Could be that Shrum had it destroyed if he realized that Tim had found it."

"It's possible. It's definitely where Tim was headed, but you saw where we found his body."

"Placed for maximum impact, I suspect. Not just for you but for other drug lords."

"It makes sense, I suppose. Even if Shrum's not a major player, he probably thinks he is. Or at least he has designs on climbing the ladder."

"And if he's got to keep a strong force on the main entrance to his compound, he might not want to expend an equal number on his back door. Especially now that it's no longer a secret. Better to just close it once and for all."

As if to underscore his words, the trees ahead of them parted, and a stark wall of fallen rock filled the path in front of them.

"Looks like you're right." Sydney sighed, frustration welling.

Avery bent, ran a hand across the rocks at his feet, then lifted his fingers to his nose. "I can smell powder residue. Someone definitely blew these rocks."

"So now what?" Sydney asked. "We're back to walking in waving the white flag?"

"I don't think we're quite ready to go there yet." He pushed to his feet, dusting his palms against his pants legs. "Although under the circumstances, it's still got to be an option. But let's move closer to the main entrance first and do a little reconnoitering."

Half an hour later, they'd made their way to the rocks guarding the entrance to Shrum's compound. Two outcroppings of limestone and granite stood sentry to an opening that was barely more than a crevice.

"Welcome to the front door," Sydney said, from the shelter of the copse of ferns and saplings they'd chosen for cover.

"I'm not seeing movement," Avery replied, lifting his field glasses for a closer look.

"My intel puts the main force on the other side. A guardhouse, usually with three or four men. It's set back from the entrance a bit." She reached into one of their bags and produced the schematic she'd brought with her. "This isn't verified, of course, but from what we could see, this is the basic layout."

The passageway was indeed narrow, stretching about fifty feet before opening out into the narrow canyon that housed Strum's compound. Horseshoe-shaped, the canyon was surrounded by rocky hills lined with ancient trees, the jungle almost obscuring where the canyon ended and the hills began.

The outpost itself sat at the end of the canyon. A semicircle of stone buildings. Aside from the guardhouse just beyond the opening, there appeared to be no additional fortifications. Only a clearing through the trees and a rough road that led back to Shrum's compound.

"Two of us, four of them. Not bad odds."

Sydney couldn't help but smile. Avery had cojones. She had to give him that. "Unfortunately there's more," she said, sobering as she continued. "There are another two guards patrolling the perimeter out here. And on top of that, two more out here somewhere, on point. Keeping watch."

"My money is on the trees." He nodded up at the towering coconut palms as well as the ancient teaks. "It'd be easy enough to set a sniper up there. If not that, then maybe the rocks themselves."

Sydney shot a look at the outcroppings. One of them stood almost erect on its own, like a dagger thrusting fifteen or more feet out of the earth. The other folded into the surrounding hills, making it seem more like a half-buried statue. But like the first, it rose high into the surrounding trees.

Vines laced their way up both sides, leaving the rock moisture-slick and shining in the half-light. The roots of an ancient banyan tree curled around the base of one outcropping like a python squeezing its dinner. And the branches of a mahogany tree arched down over the opening like a shield.

"What about up there somewhere?" She pointed toward the

rocky sentries. "Seems like that'd be a good spot for a sniper too."

"Roger that." He lowered the glasses and handed them to her. "I'm not seeing any movement at all. Have a look and see if you can find something."

She lifted the binoculars to her eyes and scanned first the surrounding treetops and then the outcroppings. Besides the undulation of leaves and branches and the never ending patter of the rain, there was nothing visible.

"I don't see anything either, but that doesn't mean that they're not there."

As if to refute the statement, something shifted and caught the dappled light, reflecting for a moment. Sunlight on metal.

"Wait," Sydney said with a frown. "Over there, between the mahogany and the rocks." She handed him the glasses, her gaze still fixed on the spot just above the opening. For a moment, there was nothing. And then again, there it was, a quick flash.

"That's the barrel of a gun. I'd make book on it."

"So we know there's at least one sniper. And given his position, I'm thinking walking in through the front door isn't looking all that hospitable. My guess is he's all about shooting first and asking questions later."

"Agreed. And if there's one—there's got to be another." He lifted the glasses again, scanning the tree line. "There." He nodded with satisfaction, pointing to a rain tree just to the south of their position. He handed over the binoculars, and she took a look.

At first, it seemed like there was nothing to see, but then the wind rattled the trees and the branches shifted, revealing the dark wood of a platform and the shadowy figure of its occupant.

"Okay, so we've got two shooters," she said, lowering the glasses.

"And according to your intel, two on the perimeter. Any idea how long it takes them to make the sweep?"

"No. All I got was that they were there. But for obvious reasons, they're not patrolling too far. I mean, the compound is ringed by the hills. So this really is the only way in."

"Well, if that's true, then they should be showing their faces pretty damn soon. We've been here ten minutes or so. Can't imagine they're more than fifteen out and back."

They both looked back at the crevice marking the opening. Sydney could feel the pounding of her heart as they waited. One minute, two. And then just as she was marking the third, a man carrying an M60 emerged from the brush, walking over to the entrance, speaking into a radio at his shoulder. Another minute passed and a second man, coming from the other direction, walked into the tiny clearing also carrying a machine gun.

The two men conferred for a moment, signaled something to the man in the tree, and then parted company, each going back the way they had come.

"Considering that they weren't here when we arrived, I'm guessing we've got between fifteen and twenty minutes before they return," Avery said.

"So what do you want to do? I mean, it would be easy enough to take them out when they come back, but then we'd still have to deal with the snipers and whomever is on the immediate other side. Not to mention that we'll most likely have alerted the whole damn compound. And if you're right about their orders to shoot, the odds of us making it to Shrum seem pretty damn slim."

"All true. But that doesn't mean we're out of options."

She smiled, her gaze meeting his. "I'm liking the sound of that. Although the last time you said that sort of thing, my boat wound up blown to bits."

"But we came out of it alive." His lips quirked upward in a half-smile, her gut clenching in response. Damn it, the man had a way of getting to her.

"Point taken," she said, pushing her emotions aside. "So what do you have in mind?"

"If we can rig a distraction and pull the snipers off their perches, we might have enough time to get through the opening."

"But what about the guys we just saw?"

"We time it right, they'll be far enough out of range to allow us the time we need to get through."

"And the people on the other side?"

"According to your plans, we've got fifty yards or so before we're spotted. So we'll use that time to figure out our next move. We've got the undergrowth to use for cover. And all we have to do is figure out how to skirt the front guard. And then how to get to Shrum inside the compound."

"You make it sound so simple."

"Well, it's definitely a gamble. But I'm thinking it beats the white flag."

"So what's the plan for a distraction? I'm hoping you're not counting on me to bring on the Siren's call."

"I wouldn't bet against that approach," he said with a grin, his eyes traveling slowly from head to toe and back again. "You've definitely got the goods, but I'd rather not put you directly in the line of fire. Better to rig something that'll grab everyone's attention without actually posing a direct risk to either one of us."

He reached into his go-bag and produced a cylindrical grenade. A flash-bang.

"You certainly came prepared." Sydney couldn't keep a note of admiration from her voice.

"A parting gift from my munitions expert. She's big on being prepared for every opportunity."

"What else have you got in there?"

"Just a couple of hand grenades and the guns you took off the boat. I'm figuring we can rig some of the ammo and use a grenade to set off a second explosion. Make them really think they're under attack."

"It just might work. But we'll have to be careful. The ground is saturated, and between that and the rain, it could be difficult to get the ammo to ignite."

"Worst-case scenario, we'll just go with the flash-bang and the grenade. But to make it work, we're going to have to separate. We need the explosions to come from both sides. Convince them that there are more than just two of us out there."

"Just tell me what to do."

Chapter 9

Avery moved silently through the trees, skirting the one holding Shrum's henchman, resisting the desire to climb up there and take the bastard out himself. If he failed, Sydney would be on her own. Better to stick to the plan.

After waiting for the two guards on the ground to meet and set off again, Sydney had taken the flash-bang and one of the three hand grenades and headed south. The plan was for her to pull the pin and throw the stun grenade at the appointed time, and then get the hell out of Dodge. The grenade was meant to be a backup.

Meanwhile, Avery was heading north—hoping to set up an identical show of fire power, this time rigging the ammo to blow when the grenade made contact and, if that failed, to simply throw his backup as far away from the gate as he could. As soon as Sydney detonated, Avery would follow suit, and then the two of them would double back and meet just inside the opening to the canyon. It was a risky move, and one that admittedly could end in failure, but it was their best shot at getting through the opening undetected.

All that remained was for everything to proceed as planned.

After successfully circling around the sniper, Avery covered the rest of the distance with ease, glancing down at his watch to be sure that he still had the time he needed to get things set. Just under five minutes.

He strode into a small clearing and knelt beside a waist-high boulder, the center slightly concave, making it the perfect mixing bowl. Working as quickly as his fingers would allow, he lined the rock's indentation with a piece of plastic torn from the inside of the go-bag. Then he emptied gun powder from several of the ammo cartridges onto the plastic. After adding several live rounds in addition to the gun powder, he laid a grenade on the top after carefully tying a thin length of twine to the pin.

Moving slowly backward, Avery straightened the length of twine until it was taut and then settled behind the trunk of a rosewood to wait for Sydney's explosion. Watching the seconds tick down on his watch, he held his breath. One Mississippi, two Mississippi, three...

The jungle lit up with the sound and fury of the flash-bang, and Avery yanked hard on the twine, the little rope resisting for a second and then the pin flying free, the grenade exploding as a rush of fire whooshed upward into the jungle canopy.

Springing to his feet, Avery ran through the trees, heading back to the opening, knowing that they had only seconds before reinforcements arrived and attention returned to the crevice. As he rounded the corner, he saw one of the guards just off to his left, the man sprinting through the bushes toward the second explosion, his path taking him right onto a collision course with Avery's.

Switching course quickly, Avery ducked to the ground and lobbed his second grenade in the opposite direction, the jungle exploding again with sound and light. The guard responded immediately, his path shifting away from Avery's, and in seconds, Avery was back on his feet and running full out for the opening.

He burst through the undergrowth and cut across the small clearing, ducking behind the rocks just as the other guard stepped from the trees. Holding position, he waited, eyes on the man as he rushed past, heading for the site of Sydney's explosion. So far so good.

Turning away from the opening, Avery quickly searched the narrow passageway for signs of Shrum's men. But although he could hear raised voices from somewhere on the far side, there was nothing in the immediate area that presented a threat.

There was also no sign of Sydney.

Avery swallowed a curse, realizing that wishing Sydney out of danger would not make it so. And although he'd wanted to stop her from going on her own, he'd known that their best option was to set off the explosions simultaneously. Besides, she was trained for this kind of thing. Every bit as much a professional as he was. Still, if anything happened to her...

He pushed away the thought and moved farther into the passageway, the rock walls and the overhanging trees making it hard to make out any detail. The shadows were welcome, an easy way to blend into the background and escape detection. From outside the opening, he heard one of the guards yelling, and just above the towering rocks, he could still see a plume of smoke rising from the site of his detonation.

Where the hell was Sydney?

Out front, he heard a commotion and then the explosion of another grenade. Sydney's backup. Moving on a rush of adrenaline and instinct, Avery pulled his rifle and headed back out the opening, his only thought to make it to Sydney in time.

After the dark of the passageway, the dappled sunlight forced him to slow his forward motion, his eyes fighting to adapt to the brighter light. At first he thought he was still in the clear, but then he saw movement at the edge of the trees. He lifted the rifle, already sighting the shot, but then lowered it quickly as Sydney emerged from the trees, hands held high, her expression a mixture of chagrin and apology.

Three men walked behind her, all of them armed, and one of them pointing his weapon at Sydney. No way in hell could he take the men out without signing her death warrant. Slowly he lowered the rifle and threw it to the ground, then he slipped off the go-bag and raised his hands.

* * *

"You should have taken them out when you had the chance," Sydney said, trying to contain her surging anger. She didn't actually blame Avery. He'd made the only choice he could have under the circumstances. But that meant the reason they were in this mess was because of her. If she'd just kept a better eye out, maybe the bastards wouldn't have managed to get the drop on her.

"I couldn't take the chance of you getting hurt." His voice was patient. As if being locked in a dank cell dug into the side of the hill was an everyday occurrence. If he was angry, he showed no sign of it. Which somehow only made her feel more agitated.

"I'd have managed." The words were a lie. He knew it. And she knew it. But the truth did nothing to soothe her rattled nerves. "Besides, what were you doing coming back out of the opening? You'd made it. All you had to do was stay hidden."

"I heard the commotion and then your final grenade. I knew there was trouble. On my team, we don't leave a man down. No matter what the operation calls for."

"I know." She stopped pacing and ran a hand through her hair. "I just feel like this is all my fault. If I had been more careful, then maybe we wouldn't be stuck in this hole."

"Well, the way I look at it, we've still managed to achieve our goal. We're in Shrum's compound. And when he finds out who we are…"

"He'll shoot us then." She slammed a hand against the door and then winced as pain shot up her arm.

"Are you always this negative when the chips are down?" The teasing tone in his voice actually made her smile, and some of her anger dissipated. He had a way of doing that. Disarming you when you least expected it.

"No. I guess I just feel guilty for screwing up."

"But you didn't. It just didn't play the way we wanted it to. We knew there was risk going in. It could just as easily have been me as you."

"Now I know you're full of it. You would never have allowed yourself to get caught."

"Sydney," he said, striding across the cell, his size dwarfing the space, "it wasn't your fault." He cupped her chin in his hand. "You followed my orders to the letter. If anyone is at fault, it's me. I put you in a position of danger. But either way, it doesn't matter. It's not about blame, it's about accepting the situation and making sure we get out of it alive."

She nodded, her gaze locked with his. And for a minute, she forgot to breathe, but then he released her, and she took a step back, needing the distance.

"As I said before, the whole reason for being here is to talk to Shrum. And our getting captured has put us in position to do just that." His smile was warm, his teeth bright against the gloom.

"Without weapons or gear." She crossed her arms, trying her best not to give in to his charm.

"He'd have taken them anyway. Give yourself a break, Sydney. There's nothing to be gained in beating yourself up. And believe me, if I thought you deserved it, I'd be the first in line to let you know."

That much she did believe. Avery called it the way he saw it. But that didn't negate the fact that she'd managed to get them caught. Still, he was right. Best to suck it up and move on. There was nothing to be gained in giving in to self-pity.

"All right, fine. So what do we do next?" she asked, her gaze moving around the tiny room. The walls were earthen, shored up with large pieces of timber. It reminded her of an old silver mine she'd visited once when she was a kid.

The metal door was secured from the outside with a tiny opening serving as the only window to the outside. So far there hadn't been much to see. Just the man standing guard and the occasional passerby, everyone armed to the teeth.

"Unless you've got a shovel hidden somewhere, I don't think we're going to dig out. And we're sure as hell not going to get through that door. So I think the best thing we can do right now is sit tight."

"And wait for them to kill us?"

"If they wanted us dead, we'd already be there. The very fact that we're here and alive indicates that they've got something else in mind for us. Since the only one here who could possibly recognize me is Martin, I'm guessing they're thinking ransom. Or if they've recognized you, then maybe they're hoping to trade your freedom for an agreement to transport their drugs."

"Either way, we're fucked." She was back to sounding mutinous. He opened his mouth to respond but she held up her hand.

"I'm sorry. I'm just pissed because I got caught. I don't like losing."

"Neither do I, but I also believe in cutting my losses. So let's concentrate on turning this to our advantage. If their angle is to get you to act as a courier, then I say we go with it."

"But I was expressly told not to go down that road."

"And you're going to choose now to toe the line?"

"Okay, maybe not," she agreed grudgingly. "But how does my agreeing to play ball help us achieve our goal?"

"If you hold out for an audience with Shrum, it gets us in front of him."

"Couldn't you just tell the guard who you are?"

"I'd rather hang on to the element of surprise. If he realizes I'm here and Evangeline is alive, then there's a damn good chance that he'll sequester her somewhere. If I can catch him off guard, I've got a better chance of getting at the truth. At least I hope to hell I do."

"So we wait." She sighed, sliding down the wall to sit on the floor, elbows on knees, her face in her hands. She heard him moving across the room, but was still surprised when he sat down next to her, an arm sliding around her shoulders.

"It's going to be okay."

It was so damn tempting to give in. To lean against his shoulder and revel in his strength. She honestly couldn't remember the last time someone had just held her. With no ulterior motive, no desire to do anything except give comfort. Her father wasn't a touchy-feely kind of guy, and her mother's idea of nurturing was tough love. Chin up and carry on.

So the idea of surrender was seductive. But at the end of the day, she was her mother's daughter. And she'd made it this far by depending on herself. And just because something in Avery

Solomon spoke to some deep part of her soul, it didn't mean she had to melt in a puddle every time the man touched her. So she squared her shoulders, lifted her head, and pulled free.

"Tell me more about Shrum. You said that the two of you had a falling-out and that you stopped working together, but how did he go from a CIA operative to drug runner? I know it's a fine line we walk, but most of the time we manage to keep our balance."

For a moment, she thought that Avery wasn't going to answer, the only sound in the tiny cell the rise and fall of their breathing.

"Assuming the photograph I have is a fake, and that the truth as I know it is still the truth, then I think the bottom line is that Evangeline's death drove Shrum over the edge."

"But she was your wife. Surely if anyone had the right to lose it, it was you."

"Oh, believe me, I did my share of grieving," he said. "But with Shrum it was different. He was always the kind of man who pushed the envelope, dared the odds. It's part of what made him a successful operative. But he always knew when to pull back. When to stop. But when Evangeline died, it was like a switch turned off. He just didn't give a damn anymore."

"What about you?"

"I wanted answers. And I wanted revenge."

"So you and Shrum started in on each other."

"For a short while." He nodded. "It wasn't pretty either. And worse, it jeopardized our missions. But then I realized the best thing to do was walk away. Revenge doesn't do anyone any good. It sure as hell wasn't going to bring my wife back. So I pulled some strings and got myself transferred stateside. It was the first of my stints with the Pentagon."

"And Shrum?"

"He disappeared. Just like that. Fell off the grid completely."

"So he must have already been planning his exit," she said with a frown. "I mean, I get being pissed off and maybe even not wanting to go on, but losing someone you love doesn't make you give up on your country."

"It does if you believe your country let you down. Shrum was convinced that there was more to the bombing than was initially reported. And although he pressed the CIA to investigate, they refused. Saying that it was a military matter and out of our purview."

"But you must have been pressing as well."

"I was," he agreed. "But I also realized that there was a real possibility that we'd never know what really happened. Roadside bombings were almost a daily occurrence at that point in Iraq. And back then, we weren't as sure of who the various insurgencies were. No one stepped forward to take responsibility, and I was never able to dig up anything to help identify who did it."

"And was Shrum right? Did our government stand in your way?"

"Not in my way, no. But it would have been damn near impossible to stop me. However, they weren't helpful. Partially because they were trying to contain public opinion in the States, which meant underplaying civilian casualties. As I said, this was long before embedding journalists with the troops was the norm."

"So do you think they actually covered up evidence?" she asked, still trying to put the pieces together.

"It's possible. That kind of thing definitely does happen. But as my rank rose within the CIA, I had access to more and more information, and I never found anything new."

"But you kept looking all those years. And no matter what the real truth was, you never walked away from the Company."

"We all have to find our own path. I, more than anyone, understand Shrum's pain. It's what drove us apart."

"So how did he wind up in Myanmar?"

"To be honest, I have no idea." He shrugged, shaking his head. "At first he was completely off the grid. Then years after that, I began to hear rumors. See position papers speculating that he was a new player in the drug trade. Then suddenly he resurfaced here."

"And no one cared? A former operative opens shop in the middle of the Golden Triangle and Langley just turns the other cheek? Give me a break. Why not burn him?"

"That's the sixty-four-thousand-dollar question, isn't it?" He raised his eyebrows, his expression skeptical. "But my guess is that it just wasn't worth the effort. Hell, maybe they were thinking the whole thing would take care of itself. Or maybe they've got some kind of under-the-table agreement with the man. I don't know. And frankly, until Harrison found that photograph I didn't give a damn."

"And now?"

"Now I want the truth. If all of this has been a lie and my wife is still alive, then I need to know why. And if Shrum had a part in it, I'll see that he pays."

"And if she's dead?" Syd asked, pretty certain she already knew the answer.

"Then I'm going to find out who the hell it is that's been yanking my chain and I'm going to hunt the bastard down and kill him."

Chapter 10

Avery woke to find Sydney nestled into the crook of his arm, her head resting on his chest. In repose she looked every bit as beautiful, but also more vulnerable, as if in sleep she'd let her guard down. And even though he had no right, he felt protective. As if he were tasked with watching over something particularly precious.

It was a ludicrous thought, but there you had it. Here in the middle of the jungle, surrounded by enemies, with the question of Evangeline's fate hanging in the balance, he was holding another woman, one who not only intrigued him but touched him on a level he'd forgotten even existed.

Guilt washed through him, and he tried to move his arm, but Sydney just mumbled something in her sleep and nestled closer. He smoothed her hair, his fingers savoring the silky feel of each strand. She sighed, her hand splayed across his chest as if she were measuring each breath—or holding his heart.

He shook his head, ashamed at his flight of fancy. She was sleeping. And he was here to find the truth about his wife. And no matter the answer, he couldn't—wouldn't—take advantage of

Sydney. She wasn't the kind of woman to give her heart easily. And he knew enough to know that she saw in him something he wasn't certain really existed. The part of him that could love had died a long time ago. And he had never even considered going down that road again.

Until now. The little voice in his head taunted him. And he forced his mind to the situation at hand, ignoring the heat from her body as she pressed against him in sleep. Save for a single shaft of pale light from the slit in the door, the room was shadowed, the air clammy and stale. He couldn't tell what time it was, but figured from the light that it had to be just past dawn.

There'd been a guard on duty all night. They hadn't been able to see him clearly through the makeshift window, but they'd heard him. So they'd both agreed to take turns keeping watch, until finally they'd both succumbed to sleep. Based on their intel and what he'd observed coming in, the outpost was well garrisoned. At least twenty, maybe thirty men. Whatever the hell Shrum was up to, he'd worked hard to make sure the place was damn near invincible. Which meant that there was probably something to hide.

Evangeline. Avery patted the pocket where he kept the picture. Soon, he told himself, soon all of this would be behind him. One way or the other he'd have the truth. And hell, who knew, maybe it really would set him free.

Outside something rustled, voices carrying into the room. Sydney sat up with a start, her eyes going wide when she realized where she'd been. For a moment, her eyes sparked with something that twisted Avery's heart, but then just as quickly, it was gone and she sat up, her professional façade dropping firmly into place.

"What's happening?" she asked, her voice still hoarse from sleep.

"I don't know," Avery said, pushing to his feet, then reaching out to help her up. "But I'm betting it's not a welcoming party."

He stepped forward, using his body to shield her as the bar on the door groaned and lifted, the door swinging slowly inward. Two men, both armed with machine guns, entered the room. The first man, clearly a local, was sporting an angry frown and a horrific bruise stretching from his left cheekbone all the way to his temple. The second stood in the doorway, the sun behind him leaving only his silhouette.

As the first man walked closer, Sydney sucked in a sharp breath, fists clenching at her side. Instinctively, Avery moved to block her further. But Sydney shook her head, stepping up beside him, one hand resting on his arm, her gaze locked on the man with the bruise.

"I see we meet again," the man said, his English broken but understandable. "Only this time I hold all the cards."

"That's pretty much what you thought last time," Sydney said, her eyes spitting fire. "But that didn't turn out so well for you did it?"

The man lunged forward, anger mottling his face, but before Avery could react, the second man stepped into the cell.

"Let it go," he said with a wave of his hand. "She's not worth the effort. Besides we've got our orders."

"Orders?" Sydney choked out, her face awash with confusion and surprise. "What in the hell are you doing here?"

Avery frowned and then recognized the man from the first night in the bar. The Englishman. Edward. He'd believed he was Sydney's friend. Judging from the look of betrayal on her face, she had thought much the same.

"I'm working," Edward replied. "Which is what you could have been doing if you'd only agreed to play along." The man was smiling, but the gesture didn't reach his eyes.

Avery inched forward slightly, keeping Sydney to his left, safely out of Edward's reach.

"With what?" She scoffed. "A drug lord. Thanks, but I'll pass."

"Fine." Edward shrugged. "Your loss, my gain."

"But you don't have a boat. Hell, you don't have any-thing—except a press pass. If that's even real. What have you got to offer Shrum?"

"Information. You and your buddies talk a hell of a lot when you've had a couple of drinks. I just remember what you say and pass it on."

"So you've been spying on us?" She made another move for-ward, and this time it was Avery who covered her arm with his hand. She stilled instantly, but he could feel the tension radiating through her.

"It was like taking candy from a baby most of the time. Espe-cially your friend Tim."

Avery tightened his hold, Sydney's anger almost a palpable thing now. "It was *you*," she whispered. "You told Shrum that Tim was coming. You're the reason he's dead."

"Tim made his own bed. I just sped it all along a little bit. Did he tell you what he was really doing here? He wasn't exactly who he made himself out to be, you know. Or maybe the two of you were in it together?"

Clearly Edward had no idea who Sydney really was. Which meant that most likely neither did Shrum. It might keep her alive if she continued to play along. But that wasn't going to happen if Edward kept taunting her. Standing beside her, Avery could feel her rage building to a fury.

"I—" Sydney started, but Avery cut her off, moving now to stand firmly in front of her.

"I can assure you that this woman had no idea who Tim really was."

Edward's attention snapped to Avery, his eyes curious. "And how would you know that?"

"Because he was a professional and he'd never have shared that kind of information with a civilian."

"He might if he wanted to get in her pants." Edward sneered, and Sydney moved around Avery, her fist already flying, but Avery managed to snag her wrist, bringing her hand in close to his side.

The man with the bruise lifted his machine gun menacingly, and Edward laughed, waving his partner off. "She really is a spit-fire. Pity she thinks she's better than the rest of us. Even old Tim couldn't get her to give him a second look, and the poor man was besotted."

This time Sydney's soft whimper was full of pain, and Avery swore that, given the chance, he'd see this man dead. "Doesn't matter what Tim felt for her—he told her nothing."

"But you seem to know everything. And why, might I ask, is that? You're bloody hell not MI6."

"No. But Tim and I shared similar interests—if you take my meaning."

The man's eyes traveled the length of Sydney's body, his gaze appreciative, but then he sobered, his attention back on Avery. "So you're a spook too? I should have guessed. You look the part. So why are you here?"

"I've got business with Shrum."

"Funny way to approach it, trying to blow us all to hell."

"Just wanted to get your attention long enough to get inside.

And it almost worked." Avery shrugged, his fingers still curled around Sydney's wrist.

"*Almost* being the operative word. And what about her?" Again his gaze turned a bit lecherous. "Why should I believe she's innocent?"

"I didn't say she was innocent." Avery's smile was slow and sure, intentionally possessive. "Let's just say she's in it for the money. Like you. And it just so happens, I was offering a better deal than Shrum. But that doesn't mean she knows why I'm here. Although now, thanks to you, she knows what I do."

"Doesn't matter anyway. You're both dead."

"We'll just wait and see, shall we?" Avery said, keeping his voice intentionally nonchalant. "I'm assuming you're here to take us to see your boss?"

Edward took another step forward, his hand tightening on his gun. And for a moment, Avery thought he'd read it wrong, that the two men had actually come to kill them, but then Edward reached out and shoved him forward.

"Fine. If you're in a rush, it's your funeral."

The second man grabbed Sydney by the arm, his grip bruising, but there was nothing Avery could do about it. If they were going to get out of this alive, he needed to hold his hand and play his cards when the time was right. He just prayed that Sydney understood.

Ten minutes later, after being marched through Shrum's encampment, they were being led down a tiled hallway in his residence, the opulent furnishings at odds with the dire poverty of the surrounding countryside. Clearly, no matter how small a player, Shrum had found success in working for the other side.

The number of their guard had grown to five. All of them heavily armed. Sydney was walking in front of him now, her back ramrod straight, her chin held high. The greasy little guard still held her arm, but it was more like she was pulling him along. Avery suppressed a smile, not surprised that Martin would have wanted Sydney to play for his team so badly. She was clearly a valuable asset. But not one that could be manipulated.

Damn good thing she was on Avery's side.

Two large doors at the end of the hallway were open, and the men ushered Sydney and Avery inside. At the center, seated on a large chair that was clearly meant to symbolize a throne, sat Shrum. Although at first, Avery hardly recognized him.

The Martin Shrum he'd known had been big and brawny. Quick to laugh and hard to fool. He'd been the kind of man who could cut through the chaff and get to the heart of things before anyone else had even realized what was happening. He'd been larger than life in many ways. And once upon a time, he'd been Avery's friend.

But this man—this cartoon version of Shrum—was a shell. His skin was drawn, his eyes circled with shadows. His cheekbones were gaunt, and his frame hunched and withered. His gaze though was exactly as Avery remembered. Sharp and intelligent. Searching, probing.

"It's been a long time," Martin said, his eyes narrowing as he studied Avery. "I can't say that I expected to find you here in this part of the world. As I remember it, you were far too interested in getting ahead to get sent out here to the frontier."

"I've always gone where I was needed."

"And you think I have need of you here?"

"I think we have things to discuss."

Shrum's laugh was raspy and dry, rattling through the room like dead leaves rustling against the stone floor. "Some things never change I see. Your arrogance was always your greatest strength and your greatest flaw." He paused for a moment, working it seemed to take a breath, and then he turned his attention to Sydney.

"I see you've finally chosen a side. I knew you couldn't stay neutral forever."

Avery prayed that she'd hold her tongue even as he knew that it was unlikely. Sydney wore her passion with the ease of youth.

"There was never a choice to be made," she said, her gaze shooting over to meet his, a small smile playing at the corners of her mouth. "It was simply a matter of making it seem as if there was."

"Ah, yes." Shrum nodded. " I see now that I made the mistake of underestimating you. I should have recognized the signs. She's not that much different from who we used to be, Avery. Fierce and proud, and *stupid*."

He covered his mouth to cough, for a moment looking much older than he actually was. Then he lifted his head again, his gaze clear, his mind obviously unfettered by whatever it was that racked the rest of his body.

"Leave us now." He waved at the men in the room. Seven in total including their original guard.

For a moment, Edward held firm, his eyes locked on Avery. "But surely you don't trust him?"

"More than I do you, actually." Martin made a shooing motion with one hand. "Go. Take the girl. As long as you have her, I'm in no danger. My friend here is as predictable now as he was fourteen years ago. It's always been about the girl with him. Always."

Avery bridled at the suggestion, but forced himself to stay calm. If Sydney were to have a chance—or Evangeline should she truly be alive—he had to keep his cool. He shot what he hoped was a reassuring look in Sydney's direction as Shrum's men ushered her out of the room, then turned his attention back to Martin.

"Kind of taking it over the top, aren't you? I mean, with the opulence and the throne. Feels a little bit too much like *Apocalypse Now*."

"Waiting for me to break into verses of T. S. Eliot?" Martin laughed again, the sound harsh against the silence of the room. "Not fucking likely. Never did go in much for poetry. All that bullshit about hidden meanings and life's great mysteries. What a load of rubbish. Sit." He waved toward a small sofa across from his chair. "And tell me why the hell you're here. It's not a sanctioned mission or I'd have heard about it. I still have an ear to the ground. So what's this all about?"

Avery started to reach into his jacket.

"I wouldn't do that if I were you," Martin said, producing a small pistol. "Remember, I know all of your tricks."

Avery held up a hand. "It's just a photograph. I came here to show it to you. But you're not the easiest man to get to." He paused, his hand still extended. "So do you want to see it?"

Martin nodded, lowering the pistol, clearly curious now.

Avery produced the photo and held it out to his one-time friend.

Martin's gaze dropped to the picture and he swallowed—the white of his knuckles the only other sign that he was affected by what he saw. "Evangeline." Her name came out a whisper—as solemn as a prayer. And Avery wondered, not for the first time, which of them had truly loved her more.

He touched the ring on his finger and steeled himself. He was here for the truth and nothing, certainly not self-doubt, was going to get in his way. "Look at the date."

Martin studied the photo, his frown deepening as he realized the importance of the detail. "And you believed this?"

"I had to know for sure," Avery said. "You know as well as I do that nothing is impossible. So tell me, Martin, is my wife alive? Is she here with you?"

Chapter 11

If she were alive, do you really think I'd be living in this hell-hole?" The bitterness in his retort caught Avery by surprise. "Besides, she loved you, remember? Not me."

"My expert says the photo is real."

"It is. Or at least most of it is. It was taken just before she flew to Iraq. We were in Germany at the air force base. Ramstein. Check the upper-right-hand corner. You can see the edge of the tarmac just outside the hanger."

He held out the photo, and Avery took it, studying it again carefully. Shrum was right. If you knew where to look you could just make out the building's opening and the runway beyond. He should have caught it. But he'd been too caught up on the idea of Evangeline being alive. Of Shrum with his wife. It was a cardinal mistake—letting emotion get in the way of logic.

"Feeling sort of foolish?" The question held no malice. Only sadness. As if Martin too had wished it to be true.

"But the date on the calendar." Hope was slow to die, and Avery realized that despite his brain telling him this was going to be the outcome, a part of his heart had bought into the idea—no matter the consequences.

"Obviously that's been manufactured."

"But you look older here," Avery insisted. "Certainly not the way I remember from back then."

"*Remember* being the key. It's been a long time. You see what you want to see. Or, I don't know, maybe they doctored my face too. But, look at me, Avery. Really look. I'm not the man in that photo. I haven't been for a hell of a long time."

Avery shifted his attention from the photo back to Martin, and for the first time, the true implications of what he was seeing sank home. Martin was really sick. And whatever it was, it hadn't just happened. There was no way he could be the man in photo. At least not now. Not this Martin.

The photo was a lie.

"What's wrong with you?" Avery asked, sinking back onto the sofa again, his thoughts whirling.

"Pancreatic cancer. How about that for a laugh? Considering all the risks I've taken over the years. Shit, I missed out on dying, by seconds, dozens of times. And then in the end, it's my own body that fails me."

"Isn't there anything they can do?"

"No." He shook his head. "Stage three. It's just a matter of time. Months now, so they tell me."

"So you've seen a doctor."

"Hell, yes. Six to be precise. I never said I was going down without a fight. But they've done all they can."

They sat for a moment in silence, the differences between them dimmed momentarily by the reality of their own mortality.

"You've done well," Martin said, finally. "I've watched your career. I wasn't kidding. I do have eyes and ears on the Company.

You can't work that long for someone and not keep abreast."

"But you gave it all up"—Avery waved a hand at the room—"for this. Why? You were at the top of your game. And you just walked away. Surely you know that Evangeline wouldn't have approved of what you've become."

"You've no idea what I've been doing. Like I said before, you see what you want to see."

"Meaning what?" Avery asked, pushing to his feet again, frustrated.

"Meaning, that for you, everything has always been black and white. Good and evil. And I'm here to tell you that it's all about the different shades of gray." Martin squared his shoulders and for a moment, Avery could see the man that he had been. "When Evangeline died, I swore I was going to find out who was responsible for her death."

"So did I. For God's sake, she was my wife. I did everything I could to find out the truth about what happened."

"Everything within the limits of what you considered right. But I went farther than that. I found a way inside the belly of the beast. A way to reach the people who had the answers. Moving drugs was my way in. And if I had to sell my soul in the process, then so be it."

"And did you find answers?"

He deflated again, his frame shrinking before Avery's eyes. "No. I came close, but then I got sicker and I…" His voice trailed off, fading to a whisper.

"So all of this was for nothing. You sold your soul, and you got nothing."

"Well, at least I tried," he said, his eyes flashing with anger. "I loved her that much."

"I loved her too, Martin, but I had to let her go."

"And how's that going for you?" he asked, looking pointedly at the ring on Avery's pinky.

"It's not easy. And seeing that picture brought it all back with a vengeance. You and me. Evangeline. Iraq. The explosion. All of it. But I'm not going to let it destroy me."

"Like it did me, you mean."

"Martin, you're a drug lord. Hell, you killed an MI6 operative."

"I did not kill Timothy Vanguard."

"He was on his way to see you. They found his body strung up outside your compound. And your man Edward implied—"

"I don't care what he implied," Shrum said, cutting him off. "It wasn't me. Timothy never came here. I swear it. And if he had, I most certainly wouldn't have killed him. No matter what kind of threat he presented."

"What about your men?"

"They can be reckless, but they would never take that kind of risk without clearing it with me. No one in my employ had anything to do with the man's death."

Avery studied his friend, looking for some sign that he was lying, knowing that the truth would be important to Sydney. "So if it wasn't you or your men who killed him, then who do think was responsible?"

"I don't have to think about it," Shrum said. "I know. Wai Yan. Or his people anyway. It's been no secret that he wants to take over my territory. But as you've seen, my position here is quite secure. So what better way to get at me than to make it look like I've killed an international operative?"

"So you're saying Wai Yan framed you."

"Absolutely. As far as he sees it, with evidence that I killed one of their operatives, the British will have no choice but to take me out. With the CIA being pulled in by association. I'm eliminated, and Wai Yan steps in and fills the void. The flaw in the plan is that Wai Yan has no idea who I really am—or was." He paused, coughing, clearly struggling for breath. "Anyway, the point being that I had no reason to hurt Timothy. And both the CIA and MI6 know that. That's why they've both tried to rein in their local people, even though it still seems as though I was responsible. They know that push come to shove, I'm not a real threat."

"But what about Sydney? Your men harassed her, sabotaged her, and, frankly, tried their best to scare the hell out of her."

"Oh please, Sydney Price has never been scared in her life."

"Well, she definitely felt threatened."

"I was right." Martin smiled, the gesture seeming macabre somehow against his shrunken face. "You do have feelings for the girl."

"She's a hell of a woman. And I care about what happens to her."

"Well, there's no need for worry. She'll be fine. I have to put on a show for my men. It's necessary. Especially now. And sometimes I'll admit they get a little carried away. But I've never intended her any harm. Hell, I kind of admire her spunk myself. We always did have a tendency to go for the same kind of woman, you and I. Looks like nothing has changed."

"Don't kid yourself, Martin, everything has changed." For a moment, the two of them were silent, the past hanging heavy between them. Then Avery shook his head, pushing himself back into the present. "You said that you chose dealing drugs as a way in. What the hell does that mean? You think the drug trade is somehow responsible for the bombing in Iraq?"

"No. I think that the people responsible are players in a bigger game. But they've got their fingers in every pot. Drugs. Arms.

Currency. Information. You name it. Drugs were just a way for me to get access."

"To whom?"

"The people who really know what happened. Look, you think that the bombing was carried out by insurgents. People who wanted to make a statement. People who didn't give a damn who was killed in the process. But what if I told you that wasn't it at all? What if I told you it was personal?"

"Against Evangeline?"

"No. Against us. You and me. We *were* responsible for her death, Avery. But not for reasons we believed."

"What the hell are you saying?"

"I'm saying someone paid a bomber to create that explosion. Someone who was specifically targeting Evangeline as a way to get payback against us."

"Who are you talking about?" Avery was leaning forward now, every nerve ending in his body firing at once as he tried to make sense of Martin's pronouncement.

"I don't know." Shrum sat back with a sigh. "I was never able to get that far. But I do know for certain that it was planned. And that somehow it was linked to us."

"And you have proof of this?"

"I've got recordings. People who admitted to me that the explosion was not what it seemed. People who swear that it wasn't an act of terror and that it wasn't about her."

"So if you have proof, why didn't you take it to someone in the CIA? Someone with the power to do something."

Martin's laugh was bitter. "I tried. But they said it wasn't enough. They even implied that it was a ploy to get back in the company's good graces."

"And was it?"

"No. I don't give a damn about the CIA, or my life when it comes right down to it. I just want to get the bastard who killed Evangeline."

"So what makes you believe it was about us?"

"I tracked down the bomber. Or at least I got close to him. Close enough to get a confession out of one of his associates. He admitted to me that the plan was to take out the woman to avenge something two CIA agents had done. He was bragging about it actually. Said that it was time for the imperialist pigs to pay."

"Did your source mention us by name?"

"No. But it has to be us. How many CIA operatives do you think Evangeline knew?"

There was clearly an element of truth in what the man was saying, but Avery wasn't inclined to trust him that far. Not without something more to go on. "But you never actually talked to this alleged bomber?"

"No." Martin was back to looking defeated. "I told you, the closest I got was his associate. I never could get a bead on him, and then the cancer got worse. And I no longer had the strength to try."

An ugly thought occurred to Avery. "Did you orchestrate this? The photograph. My coming here?"

Martin shook his head as another cough racked his body. "If I'd thought of it, maybe I would have. But no, whoever sent the picture was clearly trying to play us off against each other."

"Or bring us together." He frowned, trying to put the facts into some kind of logical order.

"You haven't said how you came by the photo," Martin prompted.

"We recovered it from a hard drive found in an Afghan terrorist camp."

"Seems an odd way for it to have surfaced," Martin mused, and for a moment, Avery was reminded of old times, the two of them working in tandem. "You think maybe it was planted?"

"It seems a fair bet, considering the fact that you clearly had no idea it existed."

"So you believe me?"

"That much, yeah. I do. I don't think I ever really believed she was alive."

"Because if she had been, it would mean she'd betrayed you." Martin sat back, folding his arms over his chest. "That never would have happened, you know. Evangeline loved you. I always wished it were different. Sometimes even pretended it was so. But it wasn't. There was never anyone for her but you. But I did love her."

"I know. And I let that fact tear us apart."

"Well, I certainly played my part. But staring at death has a way of making one face reality head-on. Maybe if I'd just come to you with what I'd found, I don't know. Hindsight is twenty-twenty and all that. The point is that her killer is still out there. And although I didn't summon you here, now that you are, maybe there's a reason. Maybe you're here so that you can continue the hunt."

"I meant what I said, Martin. It's better to let it go."

"Except that you can't, any more than I can. That's why you're here. And why you're still wearing her ring. If she was killed because of us, then we owe her the truth. Don't you think?"

"Evangeline is dead, Martin. She doesn't care anymore." It was a stark pronouncement but Avery knew it was true, just as he'd known it to be fact when he'd told Sydney the same about Tim. "But maybe we owe it to ourselves," Avery said, knowing that he was probably stepping off a cliff he'd live to regret. The operative word being *live*. "So tell me the name of this illusive bomber."

Martin leaned forward, his gaze darting around the room as though it had ears. "His name was Joseph. Joseph Isaacs."

Avery's stomach lurched, and he repeated the name. "Joseph Isaacs. You're certain."

"Absolutely, why? Have you heard of him?"

"Unfortunately. Indirectly at least, I'm responsible for his death."

"Son of a bitch." Martin brought his hand down on the table beside his chair, the strength of the action belying his emaciated state. "I was so close."

"But surely there must be someone else. Someone who helped him. Someone who can lead us to the person who's really responsible. You said you talked to an associate. What about him?"

"He's dead too. I don't know what happened. But someone must have known he was talking to me. He was killed in Damascus shortly after we met. I thought maybe it was Isaacs. Covering his tracks or something. How long ago did Isaacs die?"

"A little over six months. Ironically, he was killed in an explosion."

"And you have proof?"

"I do. The remains were identified."

"It figures." Martin sat back with a sigh. "Every time I've found something, I hit another brick wall. But at least we know for sure that he wasn't the one who killed his associate. It was only four months ago when I met with Kamaal. According to your timeline, Isaacs was already dead."

"You said his name is Kamaal?" Avery's gut was churning again, but this time with excitement. "Do you have his full name?"

"Kamaal Sahar. Do you recognize it?"

"Yes." The hairs on Avery's arms were standing at attention now. "He was the man running the terrorist camp where we found the hard drive."

"Which means that he was more than just an associate—"

Before Martin could finish his sentence, the sound of machine-gun fire echoed from the hallway outside the closed double doors.

"You set me up," he screeched, trying to push himself to his feet.

"I didn't," Avery denied as he sprinted over to pull Martin to his feet. "It's not my people."

"Then who the hell?" The windows behind them shattered, bullets strafing the floor.

"Doesn't matter," Avery said, as they dove for the floor. "We just need to find Sydney and get out of here."

"My men will have taken her back to the cell." Martin rolled onto his back, gasping for breath as another volley rattled through the room. "You need to go quickly."

"I'm not going without you." Avery's gaze moved around the room, trying to assess the safest method for exiting. Glass from the windows littered the floor. And the sound of gunfire still echoed outside the room. In the far corner, he could see the edge of a door.

"Where does that lead?" he asked, pointing.

"To the back hallway. You should be able to make it from there through the kitchen. The cell is just to the west of there."

"All right then, let's go. Give me the pistol."

"I'm too slow," Martin shook his head, holding out the weapon. "You'll never make it."

"Martin, I'm not going to argue with you."

Shrum waved his hands, still protesting, but Avery simply grabbed the pistol then picked Martin up and threw him over his shoulder, racing across the room as the next barrage of bullets hit. Slamming through the side door, he sprinted down the hall, relieved that there was at least a momentary respite from the onslaught.

He rounded the corner, his thoughts turning to Sydney. Please God let her be alive. All he had to do was make it to the cell before whoever the hell was attacking. Ignoring his screaming muscles, Avery hitched Martin a little higher and continued to run through the kitchen and out the back door. There were bodies littering the ground. He recognized Edward among them. And there was gunfire everywhere, most of it coming from the trees on the hills surrounding the compound.

Whoever this was, they were well armed and well prepared. Mindless of the danger, Avery bent to scoop up the machine gun lying beside Edward. Better to at least try to improve their odds. Shrum's pistol just wasn't going to do the job.

Dirt spewed up at his feet, and Avery straightened, shifting Martin's weight as he sped up his pace, his eyes on the open door of the earthen cell. Again a barrage of bullets strafed the ground, a stinging pain across his shoulder signaling that he'd been hit. Son of a bitch.

Still holding on to his ex-partner, Avery bent low to make it through the cell door and then set Martin on the floor. The other man's face was ashen, his eyes half closed, his hand holding his belly.

"Martin, can you hear me?" Avery asked. "You've got to stay with me."

"I'm hit," Shrum replied. "And it isn't good." He moved his

hand to show the pulsing wound in his abdomen, his torn shirt already soaked with blood. "Any sign of Sydney?"

"No. She's not here." Avery's heart sank as he tried to figure out his next move. "We can't stay where we are. We're sitting ducks, and there's only one way out."

"I haven't got any other choice," Martin said, his voice cracking as he struggled to breathe. "It's not going to be long."

"But if I can get you to someone who can help." The minute the words were out, Avery recognized their futility. Even if Martin had been in the picture of health, he might not have survived the wound. Not here in the middle of the jungle. And to make matters worse, the cancer had probably already compromised his immune system.

"Avery, don't let me be the cause of your losing someone else. Go on. Find her before it's too late."

He hesitated a moment longer, and then with a sigh, handed his old partner the pistol. "Take as many of them with you as you can. You hear me?"

Shrum nodded, the ghost of his old smile chasing across his face. "Always hoped I'd go like this. Beats the hell out of dying in bed."

"You never were one for taking the easy way out," Avery said, checking the machine gun for ammo.

"Avery?" Martin called, his voice barely audible now. Avery leaned closer so that he could hear. "If you can figure out who orchestrated this little showdown, I'm betting you'll have found Evangeline's killers." He stopped, strangled by a cough, and then with clear determination forced himself to continue, his fading gaze locking on Avery's. "Tell me you'll make it so, brother. Call it a dying man's wish."

Avery reached out to take Martin's hand. They *had* been

brothers once. And in this moment, all the things that had stood between them seemed far away. "You can count on it," Avery whispered.

But Martin Shrum was already dead.

Chapter 12

The man with the bruise, Sai, was still grasping Sydney's arm—none too gently—as he pulled her away from the compound. Apparently, in the ensuing firefight, he'd switched teams. After leaving Shrum's residence, Syd and her captors had been ambushed by four men with masks and Uzis, and in the ensuing battle, Edward had been killed.

A second group of armed men, also masked, had stormed past them into the house, spraying gunfire as they moved. At first, Sydney had thought that maybe the intruders were Avery's men. But Sai had responded to barked orders in Burmese from one of the masked men who had called him by name. The dialect was clearly Shan.

Her best guess was an opposing drug cartel, but the weapons and the MO of the attack seemed too sophisticated to have been instigated by locals. She'd seen no sign of Avery, and based on the carnage around her, she wasn't hopeful. Although maybe, like her, he'd been taken prisoner. It beat the alternative her mind kept trying to force on her. She simply wouldn't believe that Avery was dead.

It was clear that her captors were intent on getting her out of the canyon. And Sydney knew that if she was going to have any chance at all, it had to be now, before they entered the narrow confines of the passageway through the rocks. No telling what might be waiting for her on the other side.

Although she understood most dialects of Burmese, she hadn't actually followed much of their initial conversation, her mind locked instead on the idea of Avery still inside the house. She had managed to catch a few words, however. Shrum's name and a mention of retribution. But the most alarming thing she'd heard was the word *ambassador*. If these people knew who she truly was it was not only a threat to her, but to her father as well.

She had no doubt that her father would do whatever was necessary to gain her freedom, but that's what scared her. Money wasn't really an object. Her father was well-off. But if her captors were after something else—information or some kind of favor trading on his status—then her father's reputation would be irreparably harmed. Not to mention the potential danger in the release of any classified intel.

Her father sat on many boards and served on several key committees, including a joint task force that dealt with international terrorism. As such, he was privy to details about ongoing operations around the world. Locations, personnel, organizational affiliation. If intel of this nature fell into the wrong hands, lives would most definitely be lost.

Until now, the only risks she had taken in joining the CIA were her own. She'd been careful to keep any connection to her father deeply buried. But if they'd linked her to her father then the game had changed exponentially.

She'd always known it was a possibility. And for that reason, among many, many others, her father had wanted her to choose a safer occupation. But she'd rebelled. Insisting that their relationship would never be an issue. Only now, here she was, the worst of her father's fears becoming reality. And, at least for the moment, there didn't appear to be any way to escape. She was outgunned and outnumbered.

Behind her, another staccato round of gunfire filled the air. And her thoughts immediately returned to Avery. She'd been charged with protecting him. Making sure this mission went as planned. And instead she'd managed to walk them straight into not one, but two ambushes. First on the boat and then here. If this really was about capturing her because of her father, Avery would be considered expendable.

The idea made her stomach clench.

Another burst of gunfire was followed by a moment of silence, then the whine of engines overhead. As she turned to look, a huge explosion filled the air, Shrum's house erupting in flame and smoke as aircraft above strafed the house and the grounds around it with bombs. Clearly the intent was to destroy the compound. Leave no evidence. Somewhere in the back of her mind, a niggle of memory arose. A briefing she'd read.

Another drug lord's compound destroyed. Only that had been somewhere in Central or South America. She shook her head, trying to clear her thoughts. Even if there was a connection, there was nothing in the knowledge to help her now. She needed to focus on finding a way to escape. Then, if Avery was still alive, she had to find him.

"Move," Sai said, pulling her forward, his sharp fingernails digging into her skin. Instinctively, she tried to jerk away, swinging with her free arm and using a knee to try to incapacitate the man. But he was quicker, his fist slamming into her cheek, the blow sending her reeling backward. Pain radiated across her face, black spots circling before her eyes, but she fought back, still trying to take Sai down.

Syd lifted her arm, ready to strike again, but before she could make contact, one of the masked men grabbed her by the collar, literally lifting her feet from the ground. "Looks like we've got a fighter," he said, still speaking in the Shan dialect, as she squirmed against him, trying to break free.

"Perhaps someone needs to put her in her place." Sai smiled, his teeth crooked and yellowed, his breath putrid as he moved closer.

"Well, if so, it won't be you," her captor said, a hint of laughter in his voice.

"But I have a debt to settle," Sai whined, his hand rising to the purpling bruise at his temple. "The bitch owes me."

"Delivering the woman will make us all rich. So stay focused and put your grievances aside."

Syd grimaced and kicked backward, trying to hit the big man where it counted. But he only laughed again, this time dropping her in a heap on the ground and kicking her with one booted foot. Pain shot through her hip and side. But she rolled to her feet and lunged for him.

He kicked her again, and this time the blow sent her sprawling, her face scraping against the rocky ground as she gasped for breath. The masked man jerked her to her feet again, his gun jammed into her side, his breath warm against her ear. "My exact orders were to use whatever means necessary to take you alive and deliver you in one piece. But if you keep fighting me, I might choose to interpret that order more loosely. Am I making myself clear?"

Sydney nodded, fighting against waves of pain. The masked man pushed her forward, the rest of his people falling back into place. And it was only after they'd started moving again, the sound of explosions echoing behind them, that she realized that the last words had been spoken in perfect English. Which seemed to indicate something beyond a local cartel. Although there were certainly mercenaries from all over the place working the Golden Triangle. Martin Shrum a case in point. Still, she had the feeling it was important. Of course, for it to make a difference, she had to find a way out of here.

Behind her, another bomb exploded, and she winced, her mind winging back to Avery again. She'd woken in his arms this morning in the cell, and the thought that it might never happen again seemed suddenly devastating. She was overreacting. Letting emotion carry her away. She was certain of it. But it didn't lighten the heavy feeling in her heart.

Clenching her fists, she pulled herself away from maudlin thoughts. She didn't know that Avery was dead. And besides, even if he were alive that didn't give her the right to a repeat performance. Avery belonged to Evangeline. Whether the woman was dead or alive made no difference. He had already given his heart. And no amount of wishing was going to change that.

Sydney shifted her attention to her captors, again scoping the area for a possible way out. If she could manage to get hold of one of the Uzis…yeah, and if wishes were horses then beggars would fly. The words drifted through her mind, a familiar litany. One of her father's favorite verses. All she had to do was hold out. Opportunity always came to those with patience.

The group of men shifted to form a column as they approached the opening to the passageway from the canyon into the jungle. As they neared the fern-laden rocks, a shadow suddenly detached itself. Great. Another masked man. This one the size of an…

Something in the way he moved stopped Sydney in her tracks. The man swung into the light, two weapons flashing, the sound of gunfire ricocheting off the rocks and trees. Sydney's captors dropped one by one, each bullet surgical in its precision. And suddenly she was free, standing in the little clearing, staring at the big man as he pulled off the mask, his dark brown eyes filled with concern and maybe, just maybe, something more.

Avery.

She'd never been happier to see anyone in her life. Emotion surged to the surface, and she found herself fighting tears. They stood for a moment, gazes locked, and then she launched herself across the distance between them, throwing herself into his arms.

For a moment he held her, his heat soothing her like a healing balm. She cupped his face in her hands, memorizing every line and crease, the scar on his nose, the stubble of his beard, the stubborn line of his chin.

And then their lips met, his kiss hard and possessive. And for once in her life, she simply let go, taking and giving, knowing that this was what it felt like to be alive. Truly and completely alive.

Eventually, reality descended, and she pulled back, her eyes still devouring him. "You're alive," she whispered her voice hoarse with emotion. "When I saw the explosion, I was so afraid."

"I'm fine," he said, his brows drawing together in a frown. "But you're not. They've hurt you." He traced the line of her bruised cheek with a gentle finger.

"Nothing that can't be fixed." Her lips lifted in a smile. "And I promise you, I gave as good as I got."

"That I believe," he said, answering her smile with his own.

"What about Shrum?" she asked, his arms still warm around her waist.

"He's dead."

She nodded, not regretting the man's loss, but remembering that he had once been Avery's friend. "And Evangeline?" She hated that she needed to ask, but there was no other way. And she did need to know. If Evangeline was out there somewhere…

"She was never here," Avery said, a shadow washing across his face. "It was a setup. Someone wanted me here. To die—with Shrum."

As if to emphasize the last, another mortar fell, this one close to the entrance of the canyon, the rocky outcrop falling in on itself as they dove for safety, Avery's strong body covering hers, protecting her from the worst of the blast.

"You're bleeding," she said, as they rolled back to a sitting position, safe for a moment behind a stand of mangroves. The back of his shoulder was soaked with blood.

"It's just a graze from earlier." He shook his head, his attention on the burning rubble and the circling planes. "Like you said, I'll heal. Besides we've got bigger problems right now." As if to underscore the thought, another bomb exploded across the way, the rest of the rock tumbling down in an avalanche of granite, vegetation, and mud.

"The opening's caved in," Sydney said. "And the surrounding hills are full of snipers. Not to mention the planes." She nodded up at the sky. "So what do you think we should do?" It seemed natural to look to him for leadership. Truth be told, she'd follow him into hell if he asked. It was no wonder he commanded such loyalty among his people.

They were probably all a little in love with him.

The word brought her up short, and she forced her mind back to the situation at hand.

"Our best bet," he was saying, "is to try to make it to the far side of the clearing. I think the bulk of the shooters are directly above us on this side. If we can make it over there, then I think we'll be able to climb out of the canyon through that opening there." He pointed to a tree-lined crevice between two of the rocky crests. "From here, it looks like it could be a pass. But there's no way to know until we get there. And even if it is, I'm guessing the journey won't be pleasant. Martin chose this place because it was inaccessible. So you can bet on there not being another easy way out."

"I don't give a damn if it's easy. I just want to get the hell out of here."

"That's my girl," Avery said, his smile sending tingles rushing through her. Although if she were honest, it could just as easily be from the hits she'd taken. "Okay," he continued, "on my mark, we make a run for it."

"What about the planes? They've got guns as well as bombs."

"Then we're just going to have to bob and weave. We can use the rubble for cover. I know it's risky, but it's our best shot."

"Let's do it." She crouched low, her muscles tensing as they prepared to go.

A volley of bullets rang out from the hillside above them as a shadow detached from the rubble of a fallen wall. One of Shrum's men making his own dash for freedom.

"Go," Avery bellowed, as he pushed to his feet, exploding from behind the trees. Sydney followed behind him, running in a crouch, firing the machine gun she'd grabbed from one of her fallen captors.

As soon as they both hit the clearing, all hell broke loose, gunfire coming from both above them and behind them. Shrum's man was cut down before he'd even cleared what had once been the courtyard. Syd kept moving, her eyes never leaving the strong line of Avery's shoulders as he ran ahead of her.

Ten yards, twenty, forty. Bullets slammed into the mud at her feet with a sickening thwack, and she dove after Avery for shelter behind the shell of an outbuilding. A storage unit if she had to call it.

They hunkered down, using the fallen masonry as a barrier.

"I feel like a quarterback without a front line," Sydney said, gulping in air as she tried to calm her breathing.

"Football fan?" Avery asked with a grin, his eyes still on the open ground between them and the relative safety of the trees.

"I'm from Texas," she replied, working to match his bantering tone. "What did you expect? Baseball?"

"A guy can dream." Avery's smile faded as a large group of heavily armed men emerged from the trees they'd been scoping. "Shit. Looks like we'll have a welcoming party if we go that way."

"And it's not any better the way we came." Sydney nodded toward a second group also carrying machine guns, moving past the bodies at the canyon's collapsed opening. "We're running out of options."

"Well, we know that they wanted to take you alive. So maybe we should turn ourselves in."

"No fucking way." Sydney shook her head. "Even if they do take me, they'll kill you. You said it yourself. Whoever is behind this lured you in to watch you die. And in case you've forgotten, I'm supposed to keep you safe. So as long as I'm breathing, there's no surrender." She was whistling in the dark, but he smiled anyway, and her heart lightened despite the deadly seriousness of their situation.

"Copy that," he said, sobering. "So I'm thinking our best bet is to come out guns blazing and head for the hills—literally."

She nodded, knowing that there really wasn't much chance they'd actually make it. The groups of men were pulling closer, clearly aware that they were there. And one of the planes was circling back, the hum of the engine growing increasingly louder.

"Avery…" she started and then stopped—words deserting her.

"I know." He nodded, lifting a hand to caress her cheek. Their gazes met and held for one long moment, and then he lifted his gun and pointed toward the hills. "See you on the other side."

His choice of words should have scared her, but instead she felt adrenaline pumping and she popped up from their cover, already firing her weapon. Bullets hailed down upon them as they sprinted across the ground. And she knew it was just a matter of seconds. No one could escape this onslaught. Especially when there was even more danger in the sky.

The plane had moved overhead, its shadow now visible on the ground, the beating of its engine filling Sydney's ears. Except that the thought didn't make sense. Engines didn't beat. She tipped her head up and recognized the rotors of a helicopter. And then an armed man seated in the open bay of the chopper waved, and the Huey dropped lower still.

Avery appeared at her elbow, steering her forward, mouthing something about friendlies. The Huey was taking fire now, and Sydney knew they were down to seconds. Sucking in a breath, she ran for her life, bullets flying. As they reached the open bay, Avery literally pitched her up into the air. Strong arms grabbed her and hauled her aboard. Minutes later, Avery too was safely inside.

The chopper lurched as it rose back into the air, men in both doorways shooting as the Huey gained both momentum and height. One minute it seemed that they were hovering over the burning remains of Shrum's compound, bullets ringing off the helicopter's fuselage, and the next they were up and away, the jungle shrinking to a solid canopy of green.

It was clear from the back slapping and camaraderie that these people were from A-Tac. And for a moment, Sydney felt like the outsider that she was. Then Avery was there, his arm looping across her shoulders as he introduced her to his team. Nash. Drake. Tyler. Hannah. And Harrison. People who cared enough to drop straight down into the middle of a firefight no questions asked.

She'd been right about Avery. He was the kind of man who inspired fierce loyalty. The kind whose friends were ready to dive into hell for him. And Sydney knew with certainty, in that moment, that given the chance, she'd be the one leading the charge.

Chapter 13

Okinawa, Japan

Syd stood at the hotel window looking out at the rain lashing against the windows. The water running down the glass created a prism—the lights of downtown Okinawa dancing across the floor.

It had barely been twelve hours since the rescue from Shrum's compound. They'd flown to an airstrip somewhere in China and then boarded a small plane that had delivered them to Kadena Air Base.

After a short conversation via sat phone with her commanding officer, she'd been transported to the base hospital for a series of tests. The final prognosis being that, other than the scrapes and bruises on her face, she was fine. *Fine* being a relative word.

From there, a car had delivered her to the hotel, and she'd arrived at her room to find dinner waiting. After devouring everything on the room service table, she'd taken a long shower, slipped into the T-shirt laid out on the bed, and settled in to wait for word from Avery.

But she'd fallen asleep, curled beneath a blanket in the chair, only to awake in the wee hours of the night, her bruised cheek aching and her neck stiff and sore. And now she stood staring out at the rainy night, feeling like a lovesick fool. So they'd shared a kiss in the compound. It hadn't really meant anything. Only an expression of relief. The delirium of knowing they were both alive.

She'd be an idiot to think it had been anything more. And yet, she still stared at the phone, willing it to ring. Knowing damn well that it wasn't going to happen in the middle of the night. She leaned her head against the cool windowpane, feeling it shimmy in the gusseting wind from the storm.

Defiant and angry at herself for her own weaknesses, she flipped the latch and opened the window, the wind billowing the curtains as rain swirled into the room.

For a moment she closed her eyes, the smell of moisture fresh and clean. Maybe if she stood here long enough, the rain would wash away her stupid infatuation. Or maybe she'd just catch cold.

Smiling at the ridiculous turn of her thoughts, she closed the window, the rain stronger now as the full force of the storm approached. Without a jungle canopy to buffer the sound, the storm wailed its fury, rattling the window as thunder echoed against the buildings.

She'd never felt comfortable in the city. She'd always thought it must be what an animal felt like being caged in a zoo. Each species in its own special box, kept separate from all the others.

Wrapping her arms around her waist, she shivered as a streak of lightning split the sky. She was clearly in a mood tonight. Her mother would have said that the spirits were out. Her father would have said her mother was crazy. But either way, Sydney knew that there was power in the storm.

For so many years, she'd straddled two cultures. Neither one nor the other. And always she'd felt as if she were missing something—someone. Despite her talk about dismissing her parents' lasting and abiding love, the real truth was that she was afraid that she'd never find it.

And now? Now she was acting like a fool.

A clap of thunder reverberated through the room, and she shivered again, grabbing the blanket and wrapping it around her shoulders. The act making her feel not only warmer, but stronger. The adventure was over. And it was time to get back to her life. Whatever the hell that might entail. The jury was still out on whether her cover had been blown, her assignment to Laos at least temporarily over. Which could be a good thing—depending on where she landed.

Truth was, it didn't really matter as long as it somewhere far away from Avery Solomon. All she needed was a little distance, and everything would seem clearer. The man had a way of sucking you in. Making you think you were important. When clearly you were not.

She blew out a breath, angry at herself for caring so much. She was a strong woman. An operative for the CIA. And she'd always prided herself for not getting emotionally involved. She didn't need anyone. Especially not a man like Avery.

Behind her, there was a knock at the door, and her heart stuttered to a stop. So much for the independent, super-spy angle. With her heart pounding like tympani in her ears, she crossed the room, holding the edges of the blanket together like a shield. No way was she going to let him get to her again.

Squaring her shoulders and lifting her chin, she strove for what she hoped was nonchalance, drew in a breath, and opened the door. And in the space of maybe three seconds, her resolve disappeared.

He looked exhausted, and sheepish and sexy as hell. Wearing

a pair of fatigues and a khaki T-shirt, he filled the doorway, his hand still raised as if caught mid-knock. "I know it's late. But I wanted to see you."

She stepped back, gesturing for him to come in. Words seemed to have deserted her. He pushed past and then stopped, turning to face her again, his eyes devouring her. Her body tightened in anticipation, and she swallowed nervously, still clutching the blanket.

"I've been stuck at the base. A meeting with the commander. And then a satellite call to Langley. And finally, a trip to the hospital."

"Are you okay?" She reached out, wanting to touch him, but stopped herself, needing him to make the first move.

"I'm fine," he said, his voice warm like whiskey. "Actually, better now that I'm here with you." He paused, his gaze raking over her again. "You're sure it's okay for me to be here?"

And then in a moment of pure astonishment, she realized that he was nervous. Avery Solomon was actually unsure of himself. And in some weird cosmic way, his doubt canceled out her insecurities.

This was Avery. *Her* Avery. And he was here. Now. Wanting her. It was painted there on his face for anyone to see. So she dropped the blanket and held out her hand.

Her lips parted, inviting his kiss, her heart pounding, praying that he'd understand—that he wouldn't reject what she was offering. And then he was there, gathering her close, his mouth moving against hers.

At first it was a gentle kiss. Tender almost. But Sydney wanted more. She opened her mouth, drinking him in with the desperation of a woman who'd been without water too long. Her body burned for him, the fire licking at her, building deep inside until she thought it might incinerate her. His tongue traced the line of her teeth, sending tiny shivers of desire coursing through her, chasing away the doubt that threatened to consume her.

She opened her mouth, drawing him closer, meeting his tongue, tasting and teasing. The kiss deepened, and sensations exploded inside her, his lips branding her, making her his with just a kiss.

But she knew there was more, and she wanted it with every fiber of her being. She shifted, meeting his gaze. His eyes were dark with passion, little flecks of gold twirling in the murky depths of his pupils.

"Are you sure?" she whispered, needing to know.

"Yes, Sydney," he said. "With every fiber of my being."

"And this isn't about…"

He framed her face with his hands, his gaze reaching out to hold hers. "There's only you and me here tonight. I promise."

"And you want me."

His answering smile sent hot trails of fire curling through her. "Most definitely."

"Then don't let anything stop you." She smiled slowly and reached for the hem of her T-shirt, pulling it over her head.

His intake of breath was audible, and he reached out, skimming a palm along the contours of her breasts, his touch so light that she almost couldn't feel it. With a sigh, she closed her eyes and leaned forward, forcing the pressure. His fingers fluttered slightly, and then he tightened his hold, teasing each of her nipples until they were hard, the sweet pain pooling between her legs.

With trembling fingers, she pulled off his T-shirt and then they were kissing again, their bodies pressed together, moving slowly, the skin-to-skin friction deliciously unbearable. She traced the line of his shoulders, reveling in the feel of his muscles beneath her fingers.

He growled with pleasure as she caressed his skin, the sound rippling through her, increasing her desire. His hands found her nipples again, and she bit back a moan when he rubbed them between thumbs and forefingers.

"Come on, Sydney, let it go. Show me how good it feels." His whisper tickled her neck, his warm breath teasing her with its touch.

For a moment their eyes met and held, and then he lowered his head, taking her nipple into his mouth. His tongue moved in lazy circles, the gentle suction sending sparks dancing along her synapses. Impatiently, she pushed against him, and he cupped her other breast in his hand, the motion of his palm mimicking the rhythm of his mouth.

"Please," she whispered. "Oh God, Avery, please."

She felt him smile, and then his teeth closed around her nipple, the exquisite contact threatening to send her over the edge. His fingers tightened on the other breast, the combined intensity almost more than she could bear. He stroked and sucked, driving her higher and higher, each nip and pull ratcheting up the heat building inside her.

And just when she thought it couldn't possibly get any better, his fingers moved downward, teasing as they slipped inside the elastic of her panties. Something deep inside her tightened, the ache spreading through her, demanding release.

She grabbed his head then, forcing a kiss, her tongue sliding deep into his mouth, wanting to possess him as he had possessed her. Fumbling in her need, she tore at his zipper, sliding it down. Breaking contact for only a moment, he removed his pants, and watched silently as she slid out of her panties.

The bed was only a few steps away, but they couldn't wait, and he pressed her back against the wall, lifting her up so that she could twine her legs around him, opening herself for him as he thrust into her. The wind rattled the window, and the rain lashed against it as he thrust harder and harder, the two of them struggling for rhythm, striving for release.

Pleasure surpassed itself until it bordered on pain, every muscle responding to her need for release. He kissed her face and breasts, biting her nipples, and using his hands on her hips to push himself deeper—and then deeper still.

She screamed his name, certain now that she was riding the thunder, and then the world split into white-hot light, and she forgot where he ended and she began, wanting only for the pleasure to go on forever.

Shaking now from the sheer joy of it, she drifted slowly back to reality, his body hot against hers. From far away, the thunder sounded again, fading as he held her against the wall, his breathing ragged, their bodies still connected.

Then gently, he carried her to the bed, as if she were the most precious thing in his universe. And she smiled up at him, watching through layers of contentment as he lay down beside her.

His kisses now were almost reverent, as he cherished what he had moments before so violently taken. His hands and his tongue moved over her in a leisurely exploration that sent spirals of sensation dancing through her, her body reawakening to his touch, the banked heat beginning to build again.

He kissed her shoulders and the soft skin along the inside of her arms, stopping to leisurely suck on each of her fingers. Then he kissed his way across her belly, giving equal attention to the hand resting there, then up the other arm with tiny kisses that led to her ear, his tongue tracing the whorl, then drawing her earlobe into his mouth, the gentle sucking sending her squirming against the bed.

With a smile, he slid lower, kissing the tender skin of her feet and ankles, moving ever so slowly upward, ratcheting her need with every stroke, every kiss, his hands clearing the way— massaging, kneading, exposing nerves she hadn't even known she possessed.

And then just when she thought she couldn't possibly feel any more—when she was certain he'd satiated every part of her—he pushed her legs apart, his breath tickling the skin high on the inside of her thighs. One minute she closed her eyes in anticipation, and the next she was arching off the bed, his hands holding her hips in place as he sucked, each stroke of his tongue sending her closer and closer to the edge.

She grasped his shoulders, urging him onward, her mind splintering with her rising desire. Color formed behind her eyelids, burning hot, and she almost forgot to breathe.

She flung back her head, eyes open wide, body tensed as she waited to fall. Wanting nothing but to be pushed over the edge. Again and again he stroked her, driving her higher and higher until the world spun out of control.

For a moment, she floated free, and then her need for him took over. With a passion she hadn't known she possessed, she began to taste him. All of him. The salty skin at the corners of his eyes. His beard-stubbled chin. The softer skin of his neck, and the silky strength of his chest.

She took his nipples into her mouth, caressing first one then the other with her tongue, delighted when they responded to her touch. Moving lower, she sampled the smooth skin of his abdomen, tracing the ripple of muscle with her tongue.

And then her lips found the velvety heat of his manhood, and she ran her tongue along its length, pleased to feel him tense in pleasure, his hand stroking her hair, urging her onward. With a smile, she took him into her mouth and felt him grow harder, even as her own desire burgeoned, and then he was urging her upward until she was straddling him again, their gazes locked.

There would be no turning back. She was cognizant enough to know that. This wasn't a casual dalliance. Whatever they were in the other parts of their lives, they were about to commit to something here that would not easily be broken.

She raised herself slowly, and still holding his gaze, impaled herself on him, the pure pleasure of it threatening to shatter her into pieces. And then they were moving together, the friction unbearable, her pleasure and his coming together into a crescendo unlike anything she'd ever experienced. And for a moment she was afraid, frozen on the edge of nothingness.

And then she could feel his fingers linking with hers, feel his body moving inside her, and she let go, the world disappearing into the fury of their climax against the soft rumble of the dying storm.

Chapter 14

Sydney slowly opened her eyes, stretching leisurely, enjoying the soft comfort of the crisp cotton sheets. She'd forgotten how nice civilization could be. The first pale rays of early morning sunlight were slanting through the window. Avery's arm was wrapped around her waist, one leg thrown across her body, possessive even in slumber. With any other man, she would have felt trapped. A captive.

But with Avery it was different. The thought thrilled and frightened her all at the same time. They'd not talked about the future. By definition, their lives as operatives were lived day to day. But suddenly she found herself wondering what it would be like to have more. To give herself to someone completely. Always and forever.

The idea had always seemed so foreign. Like a lovely cloud completely out of reach. But now—Avery stirred, pulling her closer, his breath warm against her neck, and Sydney smiled—now the world seemed full of possibility.

She thought of her mother and father, seeing for once not the subjugation she'd always believed her mother endured but the choices she'd made. Choices that had allowed her to make a life with the man she'd loved. There had been sacrifices. But none of them worth the risk of losing the one thing that made everything worthwhile. A love that was as strong today as it had been all those years ago when a young teacher had met a village girl.

Maybe there was such a thing as true love after all.

The thought gave her pause, her stomach knotting as she looked down at the ring on Avery's little finger—*Evangeline's* ring. Clearly, he'd already found true love. And lost it. How could she ever think to fill a void like that? She could battle another woman. But not a ghost. She sighed. What she needed was to quit borrowing problems. Better to just enjoy what they had. Live in the now. She sighed, nestling into his warmth.

His arms tightened around her, and his lips found her neck.

She shivered, desire rising as she turned to face him. "You're awake."

"As much as I need to be," he said, his big voice rolling over her, warm and seductive.

She traced the line of his shoulders, reveling in the feel of his muscles beneath her fingers. His hand found her breast, and she pressed against him, all rational thought fading away against the power of his touch.

His thumb rasped against her nipple, sending shards of pleasure dancing through her, and she deepened their kiss, breathing in his essence, holding it deep inside her. His hand moved lower, caressing the skin of her abdomen, soothing and exciting her with one touch.

His lips moved too, following the hollow of her cheek, his tongue sending more fire rippling through her as he traced the curve of her throat, his tongue moist and hot against her skin.

Then his head dropped lower, his mouth trailing along the line of her shoulder, his kisses teasing in their simplicity, his hand continuing to move across her skin. His mouth found the crest of her breast, the hot, sweet suction tantalizing with its promise of things to come.

Urgency built within her. The need for something more. For connection, belonging. The part of her she kept locked away, clamoring for release. The physical pull was so strong now. So essential. Like breathing.

With desire shimmering between them, she pushed closer, grinding her hips against his, her fingers brushing the velvety tip of his penis. With a groan, he rolled her on her back, his fingers dancing across her skin, sending shivers dancing along her oversensitized nerves. And then he braced himself on his elbows, his body stretched across hers, his sinewy strength the perfect foil for her soft curves.

His gaze locked with hers, then he moved back slightly, still holding her in place, and with one long thrust was inside her. They stayed that way for a moment, linked together as man and woman, the age-old connection suddenly taking on new meaning because it was Avery.

Then he thrust deeper as she pulled him closer, urging him onward. Together they began to move, finding their own private rhythm—until there was nothing but the two of them and the incredible sensation of the dance.

She closed her eyes, letting the motion carry her away. Aware of only the feel of him inside her, filling her, their fervor increasing with each touch, each movement raising the stakes, heightening the pleasure.

There should have been fear, uncertainty about tomorrow, but instead she felt only joy. This was where she belonged. Here. Now. With Avery. Together they moved faster and faster, deeper and harder, until the pleasure exploded, and there was nothing but the power of her orgasm and the feel of his breath against her skin.

Later, when the sun had risen higher in the sky, they lay together, arms and legs tangled, her head resting on his chest as she listened to the rise and fall of his breathing. Her mind drifted. Her body, for the moment, satiated.

"We should get up, you know," she said, her inertia contradicting her words. "Your team will be looking for you."

"My team can wait," he said, rolling over so that they were eye to eye.

"But they flew half way across the world to rescue you," she protested.

"And in the process saved something even more precious."

She shivered, the tenderness in his voice almost her undoing as he reached over to tuck a strand of hair behind her ear.

"How did they find us anyway?" she asked, afraid to follow the train of his conversation any further. "I know they're good, but it's not like anyone knew where we were going. Or what we'd be walking into."

"Hannah was keeping tabs on us through other contacts here. And when our boat was reported destroyed, she tried to reach me."

"But the sat phone didn't work."

"Exactly. Which got her worried, so she called in the troops and they tracked the phone's GPS signal. Apparently with the battery on, the signal was still there, even though the phone itself didn't work. And they had the signal from your watch as well. So between the two of us, they could triangulate our position."

"And ride to our rescue," she finished for him. "Nicely done."

"As I've said before, they're a great team. Real heroes. Are you sure you're really okay?" he asked, his thumb grazing the bruise on her cheek.

"I'm fine. I promise."

"And the men who took you?" His gaze was probing now. "I take it they weren't Shrum's."

"One of them was. Sai, the man I hit in the head. Or at least he was pretending to be. But when the attack started, he was clearly part of the offensive. In fact, he's the one who killed Edward and the other men who were initially taking me back to the cell."

"And they were trying to get you out of the compound?"

"Yes. The intent was definitely to take me alive. As opposed to you and Shrum."

"Did they say why?"

"No. But I was worried that it was because of my father. They talked about my making them rich, and I heard them say the word *ambassador*."

"Which means they knew who you were. And where you'd be. Interesting."

"What about Shrum?" she asked. "Did he have insight into who might be attacking?"

"He didn't. But the attack was clearly meant to take out the two of us. And considering the coordination it must have taken to plant the picture and track my decision to come here and confront Shrum, it would have taken sizable resources as well."

"You think it was the Consortium."

"It's possible. There's definitely evidence to support that, but there also seems to be a connection to the explosion in Iraq and Evangeline's death."

"I'm not following."

"After Shrum left the CIA, he became obsessed with finding the person responsible for the bombing in Iraq. But he was having trouble getting access to the people who could give him the information he needed."

"So he made himself into someone they could trust. That way they'd be more inclined to share information."

"Exactly."

"Did Langley know?"

"According to Shrum, yes. Which would explain why they were pulling you back."

"But surely his killing Tim overrode any understanding they might have had. I mean you said it yourself, we take care of our own."

"Except that he didn't kill Tim."

"But…" she started, then stopped, trailing off, waiting.

"He said he didn't do it. That Tim never made it to his compound. And he vouched for his men as well."

"How the hell can you believe anything he said?"

"Because I knew him. And because he was pretty damn sure it was Wai Yan. After we got here, I had Hannah run a check, and the way Tim was strung up fits Wai Yan's manner of operation a hell of a lot more than Shrum's."

"Do Tim's people in London know?"

"Yes. I made sure of it. And there'll be a joint investigation. If it was Wai Yan, you can bet he'll pay."

"Thank you," she said, humbled that he'd have gone to so much trouble for a man he never knew. "Tim was a good man. He would have liked you."

"Under the circumstances, I kind of doubt that," Avery smiled, the look in his eyes making her insides turn to jelly.

"You asked about me," she said, sucking in a breath for courage, knowing she needed to ask. "How I was. But what about you? You're the one who had to face Shrum and the truth about the photograph. It had to be like losing her all over again." She waited, not completely sure she wanted to hear the answer.

"I think in my heart, I always knew the photo had to be a fake. It just didn't make sense that Evangeline would have played me like that. She wasn't the kind of woman to play games. If she'd wanted out, she'd have told me. But at the same time, I guess there was a little part of me that wanted it to be true. That didn't want her to be dead."

"Because you loved her." Just saying the words hurt, but Sydney couldn't stop herself.

Avery reached over to cup her chin in his hand. "Just because I loved her once, doesn't mean I can't love you now."

Her heart stopped, then started again, beating so hard she thought it might fly out of her chest altogether. "Are you sure?" The question came out on a squeak.

Avery laughed and leaned in to kiss her. "I've never been more sure of anything in my life."

* * *

Michael Brecht stared out the window of his personal jet, his mind racing as he watched the lights flashing at the end of the wing. So much hung in the balance. A-Tac was pressing closer, and Michael's efforts to locate Joseph Isaacs had so far turned up nothing.

Either the man really was dead or he'd found a deep hole to hide in. But Michael hadn't risen to his position of power by leaving things to chance. So he'd ordered his people to keep watching. Sooner or later the man was bound to make a mistake, and when he did, they'd be ready.

Loose ends were always a threat. And of late, it seemed that

Michael was always putting out fires. Forced to react instead of taking the offensive. Leaning back against the soft leather of his seat, he sighed. It was time for success. Gregor was right, his inner Council was getting restless. And there wasn't room for another failed attempt. Which meant stopping A-Tac once and for all.

And the best way to kill any beast was to chop of its head. But Avery Solomon was worse than a cat. Always managing to land on his feet. Not only to survive, but to thrive. Once upon a time, Avery had taken everything from him. And Michael had returned the favor. Pain for pain. But it hadn't been enough. He wanted more. He needed more.

He wanted Avery Solomon dead.

It was a way to please the Council and a way to finally close the door on the past. Two birds. One stone.

Now if only things had gone as planned. He glanced down at his watch, wondering if even now, half a world away, his enemy lay dying. If there was justice, it would be so.

In the front of the plane, Gregor sat, deep in conversation with someone on his cell phone. He lifted an arm, gesturing as if the person on the other end could see. He looked angry. Michael felt a wash of dread. A premonition that Avery had yet again managed to find an escape.

Gregor clicked his phone shut and pushed to his feet, his big body dwarfing the aisle of the jet. His face as always was impassive, but something in his eyes told Michael that his suspicions were correct.

"That was the team leader on the phone," Gregor said, without preamble. "Shrum is dead. And his compound is destroyed."

"And Solomon?" Michael asked, already certain that he knew the answer.

"He escaped."

Michael slammed his hand down onto an armrest, the resulting pain feeding into his fury. "We sent the equivalent of a small army. How the hell could he have gotten away? He was supposed to have been trapped there. An easy target from both the air and the ground."

"You've said yourself that the man isn't an easy mark."

"But we set the trap perfectly. And the numbers were on our side. He was on his own without support."

"Yes, well that's just it. He wasn't on his own." Gregor sighed, allowing himself just the barest glimmer of a frown. "There was a helicopter. It swooped in out of nowhere. Our planes didn't even see it until it was almost too late."

"And did you ID the pilot?"

"Hannah Marshall. And the gunners were A-Tac as well. Nash Brennon and Drake Flynn."

"His own goddamned personal army. And the girl? Did we secure her? At least tell me we managed to do that much right."

"Negative," Gregor said. "They apparently had her, but Solomon somehow managed to take them all out."

"Incompetents." Michael could feel a vein throbbing in his temple. "I'm surrounded by idiots. Must I do everything myself?"

"I don't think it's wise—" Gregor began, but Michael cut him off with a wave of his hand.

"I didn't ask for your opinion. I simply asked you to get the job done. And here we are again with A-Tac coming out on top."

"But we did get Shrum," Gregor said, his tone defensive.

"A dying man isn't exactly a difficult target. But at least one problem has been eliminated. He was asking too many questions, and getting too close to the truth. The issue now is how much of it he managed to share with Avery."

"But we've closed all those doors," Gregor insisted. "Sahar is dead. And there's nothing left that links him to us."

"Except Isaacs." He closed his eyes for a moment, wondering how the hell things had gotten so out of hand.

"But as far as Solomon knows, Isaacs is dead. Hell, as far as we know, he's dead. Thinking he's still alive is just conjecture. There's no evidence to support the idea. And there is data to support him being dead. So maybe, for once, things are exactly as they appear."

Michael lifted his gaze to meet Gregor's. "Things are never as they appear, my friend. And in this game, the minute you start believing they are, you're dead."

"So what do you want to do?"

"Find Isaacs before Avery does. And then use him to set a trap."

"And if we fail again?"

"We cannot fail again. Everything we've worked for—everything *I've* worked for—depends on eliminating Avery. As long as he's alive, A-Tac will continue to thwart us."

"But if we kill him, won't that mean they'll come at us even harder?"

"Not if we can turn it around so that someone else takes the blame."

"Isaacs."

"You have to admit that it would be advantageous if both of our problems could be eliminated at the same time. Especially if one could be played against the other."

"And the girl?"

"She'll be our ace in the hole. If all else fails, we'll play to Avery's fatal flaw."

Gregor frowned. "And that is…"

Michael paused for a moment, then smiled. "Avery Solomon will sacrifice anything for the people he loves. And if our intel is correct, Ms. Price has just risen to the top of that list."

Chapter 15

Syd walked into the improvised command post Avery's team had set up at the hotel and hesitated just inside the door. The entire team was gathered, Avery standing in front of a long table talking to his second in command, Nash Brennon. Harrison Blake and Hannah Marshall sat on the far side of the room, two laptops and a printer set up on the table between them. The last two team members, Drake Flynn and Tyler Hanson, were reviewing a stack of documents that Sydney assumed were intel reports on the firefight and the possible culprits. Behind them, the skyline of downtown Okinawa gleamed in the morning sunlight.

Although Sydney had worked with other operatives on various assignments, she'd spent the bulk of her career working solo. And now, watching the easy camaraderie of the team, she felt a wave of wistfulness that surprised her. Although she'd always valued her freedom—still did if she were being honest—she also envied the fact that Avery's A-Tac seemed more like a family than an organizational unit. Everyone had each other's backs in a way she'd never really seen before.

Their rescue being a case in point.

Hannah had called in the cavalry the minute she'd realized there might be a problem, despite the fact that the suits in Langley had insisted they not be a part of the operation. And now, Sydney had the feeling that they'd all gone off book, determined to help Avery not only find the culprit behind the decimation at Shrum's compound, but also the party responsible for Evangeline's death.

"All right people, let's get started. The clock is ticking, and we need answers." Avery's deep voice boomed across the room.

Everyone immediately moved to be seated, Sydney still standing at the back of the room, suddenly unsure of her place here. This was an Avery she'd not really seen—a leader who commanded the room with just a few words. And no matter what lay between them, she wasn't technically a part of the team. She hesitated, considering flight, but then Tyler smiled and nodded at the chair next to hers.

"So what's the scuttle on the attack at Shrum's?" Avery asked, as Sydney settled into place.

"As expected, no one has come out to openly take credit for it," Hannah said, pushing a pair of chartreuse glasses up higher on her nose. "But most everyone is saying it was Wai Yan."

"Problem with that," Harrison continued, his fingers moving across his keyboard even as he spoke, "is that as powerful as Wai Yan's organization is, they don't have easy access to the aircraft and firepower involved in the attack."

"That kind of thing is always for sale if the price is right." Drake shrugged, tipping his chair so that the back was leaning against the wall.

"True," Hannah agreed. "But I've been comparing it to the attack on Emilio Rivon's compound in Bolivia. And the similarities can't be ignored." She hit a key on her laptop, and two pictures flashed up on a monitor above Avery's head.

"Particularly the use of air power," Tyler said, studying the pictures. "Both compounds were strafed with bombs, the intent clearly to destroy everything in the area."

"And wipe it clean of any trace that might have been left behind from the initial ground attack." Nash frowned up at the photos, both showing similar aircraft bombing the facilities below.

"Well, it certainly makes it easier to blame someone else if there's nothing concrete to refute the idea. A few well-placed rumors, and everyone buys into the story that it was a rival organization."

"But the odds of two different drug cartels on two completely different continents using the exact same methodology to take out a rival seems a bit far-fetched," Drake said. "No matter how well-structured the manufactured intel."

"Possibly, but with nothing else to go on, my thought is that most intelligence agencies would simply write it off. It's not like Rivon or Shrum were model citizens."

"I take it Rivon was connected to another operation of yours?" Sydney asked, the brief she'd remembered suddenly taking on new meaning.

"Indirectly." Avery nodded. "We had intel that suggested he might be involved with a man we were chasing. And possibly even with the Consortium in some capacity, but before we could follow through on the information, Rivon was destroyed along with his compound."

"And you're thinking it was the same people who took out Shrum," she said.

"Exactly." Nash nodded. "Only this time, the attack was personal. The idea clearly to not only take out Shrum but to eliminate Avery as well."

"Which is totally my fault," Harrison said, his face reflecting his regret. "My friend and I went over that photo with every conceivable software, and I swear we thought it was the real deal."

"Not even you can nail it every time." Hannah reached over and laid a hand on Harrison's arm.

"Yeah, well, my mistake could have cost Avery his life."

"But it didn't." Avery's tone was firm and forgiving. And Harrison gave a tight little smile, accepting the sentiment even as he still clearly blamed himself. "And you know as well as I do that there's nothing gained in beating yourself up over something that's already done."

"Better to concentrate on putting together the puzzle pieces so that they can lead us to the bastards behind the attack," Drake said. "Then we can run them to ground and kick some ass."

"I second that." Nash smiled, but the sentiment didn't quite reach his eyes. "So first on the list is the fact that Kamaal Sahar seems to have played a role in both the placement of the hard drive in Afghanistan and the bomb that took out Evangeline's Humvee in Iraq."

"Yes, except that Martin indicated he was dead. Possibly in retaliation for talking to him," Avery said. "Hannah, have you been able to verify that? Seems like it should have come across our radar."

"I haven't got anything yet." She shook her head, her short, spiked hair swaying with the motion. "But I do have a DOA in Damascus who was never identified. It fits the location and timeline Shrum gave you. No one claimed the body, and he was buried in a pauper's grave. We're having his body exhumed now to check for identity."

"Why the hell wouldn't the authorities have checked it at the time?" Drake asked. "Kamaal is at least in our top one hundred."

"My guess is that someone bribed them to turn the other way. Better for them if Kamaal stays alive." Avery leaned against the table, crossing his arms over his chest.

"Better to have us chasing ghosts," Drake said, "than someone who might really matter."

"Well, they know it's important," Hannah assured them, looking over the top of her glasses. "And I've put a rush on it, so we ought to know something definitive soon."

"But assuming that Shrum's right and Kamaal is dead, then we're shit out of luck since Isaacs is dead, too."

"Still, we're a lot closer to connecting the dots," Avery said. "If Shrum was telling the truth, then it's possible that Evangeline's death was linked to Shrum's and my past. Something that made it worth the effort to try to lure me into a trap at Martin's compound."

"But what?" Sydney asked. "And why now?"

"I don't have the answer. But if we can find it, I've got a feeling we'll be closer to not only finding the person responsible for Evangeline's and Shrum's deaths, but also someone high up the ladder within the Consortium."

"You're thinking, beyond the obvious tie between our interfering consistently with Consortium objectives, that there's a personal angle as well?" Tyler posed the question, but it was clear she already knew the answer.

"I don't see how we can avoid it," Avery said. "We know that both Kamaal and Isaacs had ties to the Consortium. And we know that neither of them were part of the inner echelon, because they were both deemed expendable."

"The Consortium definitely isn't shy about offing people it

sees as a direct risk to exposing the inner workings of the organization," Drake offered.

"But according to Shrum," Sydney continued, expanding on Avery's thought, "both men had a direct connection to Evangeline's death. Isaacs perhaps even building and then planting the bomb."

"And Shrum believed the motivation was rooted in the two of you," Nash added. "Which seems to back up the idea that someone, potentially the same person, tried pretty damn hard to lure you into a deathtrap."

"Well, if all that's right," Tyler said, "then I'm guessing someone out there is pretty pissed off. Not only have we continued to thwart his or her continued efforts to detonate a weapon of mass destruction, we've also managed, despite what should have been a slam dunk, to keep his nemesis alive."

"Meaning Avery." Sydney felt her heart contract as she remembered just how close she'd come to losing him.

"Yeah, well, the best laid plans and all of that," Drake said. "Clearly this dude hasn't gotten the message yet. We don't go down easy."

"No, we don't," Avery concurred. "But if we're going to put an end to this once and for all, we need to act fast. Before anyone has time to regroup. Hannah, I want you to dig deep into my past. Nothing left unturned. Look at every operation Shrum and I were involved with. Especially ones where we were successful in either bringing someone down or eliminating them all together. Especially if there was arms trafficking involved." He stood up with a frown. "If this is personal, then it's about payback. Whoever this is, he wanted me to feel the same pain he did."

"So what's our next move?" Tyler asked. "Beyond researching Avery's past and waiting for verification that Kamaal is dead."

"I think I can answer that," Harrison said, looking up over the top of his computer, his gaze encompassing them all. "I had Tracy take a look at the tissue sample we took from the body found at the blast site of the bomb that killed Isaacs."

"And Tracy is?" Sydney asked, confused.

"Tracy Braxton," Tyler answered. "One of the top forensic pathologists in the country. She owns Braxton Labs, and she's a good friend of Harrison's. And good people. She helped us nail a serial killer a while back."

"Yeah, but I thought we'd already verified that it was Isaacs's body they found." Drake dropped his chair back on all four legs, leaning forward, clearly curious.

"Something just didn't feel right to me," Harrison said. "So I figured better to have someone take another look. And she just sent me the results."

"And what did she say?" Avery prompted.

"That the body they found wasn't Isaacs. It belonged to a guy named Warner Stoltz."

"And do we know anything about this Stoltz?" Avery asked.

"Just that he's a gun for hire," Hannah said, reading from her computer screen as she typed. "German mercenary. No known affiliations as far as groups are concerned. But I only just started working on it. In the meantime, my guess is that he was sent to take out Isaacs but Isaacs got to him first. He probably planted the trace we found that made us believe he was the one who died. He certainly had the expertise to set the bomb."

"Makes sense," Nash agreed. "Isaacs certainly represented the threat of a leak, especially when you consider that we destroyed his network. And quite frankly, I never really believed that Isaacs would let himself get blown up by his own bomb."

"So if the Consortium did target Isaacs, then he's probably out there on the run or lying low somewhere," Sydney offered.

"And that means he might be willing to spill his guts," Drake said. "With the proper inducement, of course."

"Well, I sure as hell don't like the idea of the man walking free after all that he's done." Nash frowned.

"It's a trade-off," Avery shrugged. "And considering the Consortium seems bent on destabilizing any efforts at a peaceful world accord, I'm thinking it's a small price to pay. But before we start debating the merits of any kind of bargain with the man, we have to find him. And Isaacs has already proved that he's adept at covering his tracks."

"Yeah, well, not as well as he might think," Hannah said with a smug smile. "As soon as Harrison texted me about Tracy's results, I started digging. And thanks to some security footage and our facial-recognition software, I'm pretty sure I've found him. He's in Scotland. On the Isle of Skye."

"So what do we do now?" Sydney asked, her gaze moving to Avery's.

"We find the son of bitch and make him an offer he simply can't refuse."

Chapter 16

Isle of Skye, Scotland

The largest island in the Inner Hebrides, Skye had a windswept wildness that bred only the toughest of men. It was here that the Clans MacLeod and Donald had been born, the ruins of their tower-house strongholds still standing testament to the tenacity of the Scottish Highlanders.

Avery breathed in the cold, salty air, his gaze sweeping over the rolling green fields dotted with grazing sheep. A few crofters' huts were scattered across the treeless expanse, their lichen-covered stones standing white against the red hills rising wraithlike behind them. Mist curled in and around the little valley, which, at this early hour, seemed completely void of human inhabitation.

With a frown, Avery centered his attention on a stone cottage with a thatched roof about fifty yards in front of them, just at the bottom of a small rise. "According to Hannah's intel," he said, turning to Nash, Drake, and Sydney, who were also watching the cottage, "Isaacs should be holed up in there. Unless somehow he's gotten word that we're on to him."

The team had taken the first flight they could secure out of

Okinawa, and after a quick stop in Germany, had boarded a second plane bound for Edinburgh. From there they'd made their way by car to the bridge from Kyle of Lochalsh to Kyleakin and on to the northwest and the cottage in the glen below them. The journey had taken just over twenty-four hours.

The rest of the team was still in Edinburgh. Hannah and Harrison still trying to ferret out information connecting Warner Stoltz to the Consortium. Tyler focusing on reporting in to Langley, who in turn would clear the way with MI5 for official sanction of Avery's presence in Skye.

Although it had been tempting to keep the operation off-book, Avery knew that there was potential for blowback if things should go south. Or, more important, if Isaacs should point to other Brits playing major roles within the Consortium. Better for once to cross his t's and dot his i's.

"I don't see how he could possibly know we're here," Nash said. "There hasn't really even been time for MI5 to have been informed."

"Besides," Drake added, "this place is out in the friggin' middle of nowhere."

"Not to mention the fact that there's no one for him to get information from." Sydney shrugged. "I mean, he can hardly call the Consortium. If we're right, they're the ones who tried to kill him. And if he were to contact anyone on our side of the equation, it wouldn't go much better. After all, he is wanted for terrorism."

"Bastard is lucky we need to talk to him, or we'd be the ones taking him out," Drake said. "We may have managed to avert catastrophe in New York, but that doesn't mean much to the people Isaacs killed."

"Or their families," Avery agreed. "But if he can give us information that will lead to taking down the Consortium, it'll go a hell of a long way toward evening the score."

"Well, I'd still rather see him dead," Nash said, pulling out his gun as they prepared to go. "But I'll settle for taking him into custody and throwing his ass in jail."

"Who knows?" Sydney offered. "Maybe someone there will do the honors for us. Even criminals can be patriotic. I'm guessing terrorists aren't exactly top of the food chain when it comes to incarceration."

Drake shot Sydney a smile. And Nash let out a laugh. Clearly, they'd accepted her as part of the team. And, Avery thought, not for the first time, how fate often turned on a dime. He'd arrived in the Golden Triangle looking for one woman, and in the process, fallen in love with another.

Second chances were rare, and Avery was wise enough to recognize the fact. This time, no matter what it cost him, he was determined not to make the same mistakes. But that didn't make it easy. His instinct had been to refuse Sydney's request to come with them. To instead insist that she head back to the States. But the Consortium had made this her battle when they'd tried to kidnap her. And he knew her well enough to know that she wasn't going to just walk away without a fight.

So he'd swallowed his fear and allowed her to come—knowing full well that they could be walking into some kind of trap. Isaacs's, or worse, the Consortium's.

"All right," he said, focusing his thoughts on the task at hand. "We'll move out on my signal. Nash, you and Drake head for the back, and Sydney and I will take the front. And no matter how tempting it is to do otherwise, we take him alive."

"Roger that," Drake said, already moving down the slope, he and Nash keeping low, using a rambling stone wall for cover.

"You ready?" Avery asked, turning to Sydney, who like Nash had pulled out her gun.

"Locked and loaded." She gave him a thumbs-up, and they too, started down the hill, in short order covering the ground between the hedgerows leading to the cottage.

It was low-slung, fronted by a brown door and two small windows. A gorse bush, untrimmed and overgrown, huddled outside one of the windows, its tightly grouped branches tapping against the glass. A battered bicycle leaned haphazardly against the wall near the door, and a large, twisted rowan tree stood in front of the other window, dark green leaves unfurled toward the rising sun. The little house, like others in the area, was built of stone, the rocks weathered to varied shades of brown and gray.

As they approached the front door, weapons at the ready, a startled fieldfare swooped out of the tree, wings thrashing as it whistled in fright. Avery motioned Sydney still, and they waited in the shadow of the big tree, but nothing else moved. With a nod, he sent them both forward again, Sydney flanking the door to the right as he took position on the left.

Again, they waited, but the silence continued unbroken. Avery reached for the door handle and turned the latch, slowly pushing the heavy door open. Moving on his signal, Sydney swung across the threshold, her weapon raised, Avery following immediately behind her.

A small hall ended with a stairway leading up to a loft or an attic at the far end. To the right was an archway opening into what served as a living room, an open book on the table next to a teacup giving at least some credence to the possibility that someone was in fact living there.

Sydney mouthed the word *clear* and then lowered her gun, reaching out to touch the cup. "It's still warm," she whispered, her gaze sweeping across the room. "And the fire is banked. I can see the coals from here."

Avery lifted a finger to his lips and lifted his chin toward the ceiling above them, the soft sound of something moving barely discernible. Sydney nodded, lifting her gun again, and together the two of them made their way back into the hall, stopping in front of the second opening on the left. Nash and Drake stepped into the dining room from a second doorway leading to what must be the kitchen and the back entrance.

Drake shook his head, indicating that they hadn't found Isaacs, and then opened his mouth to speak, but Avery motioned him quiet, pointing at the ceiling again, another rustle from above confirming the potential of an upstairs occupant. Without waiting for the others to catch up, Avery moved down the hall to the staircase. The steps were old and very narrow, forcing them to proceed single file.

Avery took the lead with Sydney behind him, and Drake and Nash bringing up the rear. At the top he stopped for a moment in the shelter of the stairwell, waiting for his eyes to adjust to the gloom. Then, leading with his gun, he rounded the corner. At first glance, the room appeared to be empty.

An unmade bed filled most of the space, a large rocker sitting across from it near the small dormered window. Light slanted across the wood-planked floor as it filtered through a pair of tattered lace curtains. And as the four of them filled the tiny room, nothing else moved except a swirl of dust motes.

"Maybe it was the wind," Sydney said, nodding toward the curtains fluttering slightly in the breeze.

"Or maybe not," Avery replied with a frown as a moan emanated from the general direction of the floor on the far side of the bed. Moving cautiously, gun raised, Avery inched forward, skirting the quilt, which had fallen off the end of the bed. The shadows were deeper in this corner of the room, and it took a moment for Avery to make out the shape of a man lying facedown on the floor near the far wall.

Keeping the gun trained on the still figure, Avery crossed over and knelt down to turn the man over. He moaned with the motion, eyes closed, blood staining the white cotton of his shirt, a pool of it on the floor where he'd been lying.

"Is it Isaacs?" Sydney queried.

Avery nodded. "He's been shot," he said, although they could all see the blood, making the statement a blinding glimpse of the obvious. "And from the amount of blood, I'd say the bullet nicked an artery." He leaned closer as Drake searched the room. Sydney knelt on Isaacs's other side, while Nash produced the sat phone Hannah had given them. "Joseph can you hear me?" Avery asked.

The man moaned, and then his eyelids fluttered open, the pain reflected there indicative of the degree of his injury. His eyes widened as he recognized Avery, his body thrashing as he tried to roll away.

"Just hang in there," Sydney whispered, laying a hand across Isaacs's brow, her touch stilling him instantly. "We're going to get you some help."

Fear faded, but he was still clearly agitated. He tried to say something but the words got lost as he grimaced again with pain, the bloodstain on his shirt spreading rapidly as he struggled for breath.

Avery opened the buttons on Isaacs's shirt, pulling the material away to reveal a gaping wound, blood spurting in little pulses from the opening. Sydney swallowed a gasp when she saw it, and behind her, Drake was shaking his head. Avery had seen sucking wounds like this, recognizing that for every drop of blood oozing out onto his belly an equal or possibly greater amount was seeping into his abdomen.

Even if helped arrived now, there was little chance that Isaacs would make it.

"Can you tell me who did this to you?" Avery asked, bending low so that he could hear the answer. "Was it the Consortium?"

Isaacs opened his mouth to answer, but only a gurgle of sound emerged.

Frustrated, Avery shifted to sit back on his heels, but before he could move away, Isaacs grabbed his wrist, his grip surprisingly strong considering the extent of his injuries. "Gre…" he started and then stopped, his breathing coming in gasps now. "Gre…" he said again, this time a little louder.

Avery leaned close again. "Tell me. Who did this?"

"Gre…Gre…gor," Isaacs whispered, and then his hand went slack, his chest rising and falling one last time as the breath left his body.

"Is he dead?" Sydney asked, her hand still cupping Isaacs's face. Avery nodded.

"So what was it he was trying to say?" Drake asked as Nash moved over to the window, talking animatedly with someone at the other end of the phone line.

"I'm not sure," Avery answered, frustration cresting. "It certainly sounded like a name. Gregor, I think. But I have no idea who that is. For all I know, it's his father or brother or a neighbor or something."

"Or maybe it's someone with the Consortium," Drake offered, staring dispassionately down at the body. "Like his killer."

"You find any trace that might help us narrow the options down a bit?" Avery asked.

"No." Drake shook his head. "There's a hole in the wall over there from a bullet, but someone dug the slug out. Might be prints. But we'll need forensic techs to find out."

"On their way," Nash said, snapping the sat phone shut. "For now it's just the locals. But Hannah's on the horn with the brass in London as we speak, so I figure we'll have a whole cadre of people within a couple of hours."

"Good," Avery said. "In the meantime, we need to be sure that no one moves the body or messes with the scene. Even the local techs. We can use them to get the basics, but we'll save the rest for the London crew."

"Avery?" Sydney called, still kneeling by the body, her head tilted quizzically as she studied the dead man. "I think maybe there's something in his hand."

Avery dropped down beside her, and reached out for the man's left hand. Carefully he pried back the lifeless fingers, and a small plastic disk dropped to the floor accompanied by a small scrap of paper.

On the paper, Isaacs had written a series of coordinates along with a date and time.

"Looks like latitude and longitude," Nash noted from his position just over Sydney's shoulder. "I'm guessing a location?"

"But for what?" Sydney frowned.

"No idea." Avery shook his head, pushing to his feet, still holding the paper. "But I'm guessing it's important."

"Wait a minute," Sydney said, her voice hushed, almost a whisper. "I think we've got a problem."

Avery spun back to her, his gaze following hers to the black plastic disk on the floor. It looked a little like a garage door opener. With a gray button in the middle. Only Isaacs's cottage didn't have a garage. And a light just above the button was flashing red.

"Considering Isaacs's penchant for making things go boom, I'm guessing that's a detonator," Drake observed, his voice like Sydney's gone suddenly sotto. "And since thanks to us, he's only just released it, I'm also guessing that it's been primed."

"Which means that we've probably only got seconds to get the hell out of here." Nash was already moving toward the door. Drake close behind.

Avery literally swung Sydney up and over his shoulder, running with her through the door and down the narrow stairs, taking the steps two at a time. At the bottom, he broke into a full-out sprint, tearing down the hallway and through the doorway, out onto the grass beneath the rowan tree.

Ahead of him, he could see Nash and Drake as they dove for cover behind the stone wall. He started to follow, still holding tightly to Sydney, but a wave of pure energy and heat lifted him instead, throwing them into the air before sending them slamming back into the ground. Behind them, the house exploded in a burst of smoke and fire, and Avery rolled to cover Sydney's body with his, shrapnel from the house raining down on them.

The air was filled with the acrid stench of the burning remains, and black soot darkened the space around them. "Are you okay?" he asked, as he rolled off her, his heart in his throat as he helped her sit up.

"Yeah," she nodded, her wide-eyed gaze meeting his. "I think so." She gave him a trembling smile. "Thanks to your quick thinking. Your saving me is getting to be a habit."

"One I'd just as soon not have to repeat any time soon," he said, returning her smile. "Nash? Are you and Drake okay?"

"Roger that," his number two responded, wiping ash from his face and hands. "Just a couple of bruises. Thank God you saw the damn thing, Sydney."

"I don't know, if we hadn't pried it free…" She broke off, the enormity of the idea hitting her hard.

"Wouldn't have made a difference," Avery reassured her as he pushed to his feet, then held out a hand to help her up. "The pressure was released the minute Isaacs died. He probably thought he'd be taking his killer with him. Only clearly he lasted longer than expected."

From the distance, Avery could hear the sound of a helicopter.

"Looks like help is on its way," Nash said. "Any chance you managed to keep hold of the slip of paper?"

"Hell no," Avery bit back a second oath as he looked down at his empty palm. "I must have dropped it when I grabbed Sydney."

"Totally understandable," Nash replied. "And I'm guessing in the moment you weren't thinking about memorizing the coordinates either."

Avery shook his head, frustration turning to anger. "I fucked up."

"Considering you saved my life, I think that's overstating it a bit," Sydney said, her smile growing broader. She was covered in soot, her teeth shining white against the black covering her cheeks, nose, and chin. "Besides, as it so happens, my memory is pretty close to photographic. Which means I've got the coordinates right here." She touched a finger to her head, and Avery swung her into his arms with a whoop.

"Now, that's my kind of woman."

Chapter 17

London, England

Y ou're going to wear the carpet out," Hannah Marshall said, as Sydney paced across the rug for the seven millionth time.

Syd stopped, staring out the window into the quiet, cobblestoned street. The team had arrived in London several hours ago, and after a debrief with their English counterparts, had set up base at an MI5 safe house in the Maida Vale district of London. A small town house on a quiet mews.

Isaacs's coordinates had zeroed in on a business complex on the outskirts of London. The date and time indicated a possible meeting of some kind this afternoon. After much discussion and a liberal amount of arm twisting, A-Tac had been allowed lead on the attempt to subvert whatever might be about to happen.

And since Sydney wasn't technically assigned to the unit, Avery had ordered her to stay in Maida Vale with Hannah. Resigned to the turn of events, Sydney had been working with Hannah to try to track both Warner Stoltz and Isaacs's Gregor. But so far, they'd hit nothing but dead ends. And the time was quickly approaching for whatever the hell Avery was walking into.

Nash, Drake, Tyler, and Harrison were with him. And she

knew that they were more than equipped to handle any situation, but that didn't make it any easier to be the one left behind waiting.

"It wasn't his call," Hannah said, correctly reading the train of Sydney's thoughts. "He never would have asked you to stay behind. It was just protocol. Mainly MI5's. They're sticklers for that sort of thing. And we've been known to go off-book before, so I'm guessing they're even more determined to keep us in line."

"It's fine," she replied, turning from the window to face the other woman. "Even if it was Avery's call, I'd have understood it. No matter what else is going on, I'm a distraction. He needs to put the team first, and with me present, that just isn't going to happen."

The minute the words were out, she regretted them. They hadn't even spoken about a relationship privately let alone publicly, and here she was spouting off to his friend as if they were a real couple. She ducked her head, feeling the hot stain of a blush spreading across her cheeks.

"Harrison is the same way during an operation," Hannah said, ignoring Sydney's obvious embarrassment. "He's constantly torn between wanting me alongside for backup and wanting to sequester me in some kind of fortress for the duration. I mostly just ignore it. Although to be honest, if I had the choice, I'd lock him away somewhere safe too. It's just the way it is when you love someone."

"But you manage?" Sydney asked, curiosity making her abandon all pretense. "I mean, the two of you together, it works? Even with both of you risking your lives?"

"Yeah." Hannah smiled, looking over the top of her rhinestone-encrusted glasses. "It isn't always easy, but part of what makes it work is that we truly do get it. Both the need to be out there on the front lines and the desire to keep each other safe. It's a balancing act. And sometimes one of us has to give. But we went into it with eyes wide open and the knowledge that we're better together than apart."

"But Avery…" she began, then trailed off, chewing her lip.

"Is Avery," Hannah finished for her. "Larger than life. We all feel that way about him. But the truth is, he's just a man. He puts his boots on the same way as the rest of us."

"Yeah, but they're some pretty amazing boots. I mean, just over the past few days, he managed to single-handedly thwart the Consortium, with a couple of drug kingpins thrown in for good measure, and save my life three times in the process."

"Believe me, you're singing to the choir. Avery has been there for me in more ways than I can possibly enumerate. He's family. Hell, he's the heart of A-Tac. I've no doubt he'd take a bullet for any one of us. But I've also never seen him light up the way he does when you're around. Never."

Sydney felt herself go warm again.

"And if you feel the same way about him," Hannah continued, "then you'll figure the rest of it out the same way Harrison and I did, one day at a time."

"Good thoughts." She glanced down at her watch. "They should be getting ready. The meeting, or whatever it is, is only a little while from now."

"I'm sure they've got it under control. For all we know, it'll be a dead end. If Isaacs was supposed to be meeting someone, it's possible they already know he's dead. Which means there won't be anyone there. And if Avery runs into a problem, he knows we're here for backup."

Sydney nodded, still not completely convinced. "I just can't help but worry that this is another trap."

"I've had the same thought. But you have to remember that Isaacs was holding the trigger to a bomb as well. He had to have been holding both at the same time, which makes it pretty unlikely that his killer left the slip of paper. If he'd attempted something like that, it seems to me that he would have been blown up in the process."

"So maybe they really will find something solid." She sighed, running a hand through her hair, exhaustion warring with concern. "It would be really nice if we could nail the bastards behind the attack in Myanmar."

"Avery said they were trying to kidnap you."

"Yeah, it looks that way. I think maybe to have leverage over my father."

"Ambassador Walker."

"You are good with intel," Sydney said with a smile.

"Well, that bit came from Avery. Have you talked with your dad?"

"Not yet. I wanted to make sure I had all the facts. I've no reason to believe he's in any danger. Just that someone might have been trying to get to him through me."

"Which is worrying in and of itself," Hannah agreed. "But sitting here fretting isn't going to do either one of us any good. Besides being my friend, Avery is also my boss, and if we don't have new information on Warner Stoltz and this Gregor character by the time he gets back, heads are going to roll. And given his feelings for you, I'd say most likely that means mine." Her smile widened as she turned back to her computer screen.

"So where are we?" Sydney asked, grateful that they'd moved onto safer topics and yet comforted by both Hannah's wisdom and support. Maybe she was going to like this teamwork thing.

"I'm cross-referencing Stoltz's name with Gregor's. Makes it more difficult when we've got only one name. And we're not even sure whether it's a first name or a surname. But if I get a hit, then maybe we'll have more to go on."

"What about Stoltz? Anything more that might connect him to the Consortium?"

"The tricky thing with this group is that we don't have any names. Or at least none that are living. Every time we get close to someone that might have answers, they manage to get to them first."

"And shut them up permanently."

"Exactly. Although nobody's perfect, and sooner or later they're bound to make a mistake. So far though, I've got a short list of Gregors with connections to the arms industry—players on both sides of the fence, legitimate and otherwise—but nothing that links any of them to the Consortium. But this kind of thing takes time. And a lot of digging."

"What can I do?" Sydney asked, looking for something, anything, to keep her mind occupied.

"Well, if you really want to help," Hannah said, waggling her eyebrows over the rims of her glasses, "you could go to the pub on the corner and get us something to eat. I've got a thing for English pasties, and I noticed they were listed on the chalkboard as we drove by on the way in."

* * *

"When people talk about the fog in London, they're not exaggerating," Drake said as they huddled in a breezeway across from the building pinpointed by Isaacs's coordinates. "I can't see my damn hand in front of my face."

"Makes it a hell of a lot more difficult to manage surveillance," Nash agreed.

"Not to mention making it feel like you're soaked to the bone without actually getting wet." Harrison shivered, rubbing his hands together for warmth.

"You guys are just babies," Tyler said. "You'd think you'd never seen a little mist."

"Hey, we're way beyond mist," Drake said, waving a hand at the shrouded street in front of them. "There's a reason they say thick as pea soup."

"So what's the play?" Nash asked, cutting through the chatter to bring them back to the matter at hand.

"We infiltrate, then neutralize anyone we find inside," Avery said, his gaze sweeping across the rain-slick pavement to the building partially masked in the heavy fog.

Four stories tall, it had stood empty for the past eighteen months, a by-product of the economic strife that had swept across Europe. The owner had defaulted on his loan, leaving the building in bank hands. But although the bank was holding the papers, it was clear from the broken windows on the first floor that the building wasn't being maintained.

"Place looks more like a crack house then an international conglomerate's headquarters," Tyler observed, correctly reading Avery's thoughts.

"Appearances can be deceiving. Bottom line, Isaacs had the address for a reason. And now it's up to us to figure out what it was." He glanced down at his watch. "It's time. We'll go on my mark." He waited as the seconds ticked down and then signaled Tyler, who was tasked with coming in through the back of the building.

She moved out, keeping low, and after no more than fifteen feet or so, disappeared into the fog.

"Nash, you're next."

His second in command nodded once, and then after checking his weapon, sprinted for the fire escape located on the south side of the building. His job was to access the roof and then enter through a service duct using the ladder there. One minute he was there in plain view and then he too disappeared into the gloom.

"All right, Harrison, Drake and I are off next. We'll check in as soon as we're in position. You'll be here keeping an eye on anyone coming and going."

"Roger that," Harrison agreed. "Besides having eyes on the building physically, I've also hacked into the feed of a couple of nearby security cameras. So far there hasn't been any activity. Although it's hard to be certain with the fog."

Avery glanced down at his watch again. "According to this, we should be right on time for the party, whatever the hell it is."

"Good hunting," Harrison said as they set off, heading across the pavement into the shadows of the overhang from the building directly next door.

"You're thinking this is a trap." Drake's tone made it clear that he wasn't asking a question.

"I think it's a distinct possibility," Avery agreed. "So we need to be ready for anything."

The two of them inched forward, covering each other's backs as they made their way to the front door of the identified building.

"Harrison," Avery called, reaching up to adjust his earpiece. "You getting this?"

"Copy that." Harrison's voice was broken up by static but still audible.

"Nash?"

"I'm here," Nash responded. "The door was locked, but I managed to pick it. So I'm ready on your go."

"Tyler?" Static filled the line, and Avery tightened his grip on the Beretta he carried. "Tyler, are you receiving this?"

"Loud and clear," came the answering response. "Sorry for the delay. I thought I had company, but it turned out it was only a cat. I'm in place now. Chain and padlock no longer operational."

"All right then," Avery said, flipping on the tac light attached to his gun. "Let's go in. Everyone stay alert."

Flanking both sides of the door, Avery and Drake waited a beat and then pushed it open, and stepped inside. After the cold swirling mist, the inside of the building seemed unusually warm. The floors were dusty, and in places, the insulation showing through holes in the walls.

"Not exactly a palace," Drake said, swinging into an empty room, leading with his gun.

"We're clear in here."

Together they worked their way down the hall, finding nothing but empty offices and abandoned furniture. A couple of the offices had been adopted by squatters, refuse piled in corners. But anyone who had been living there had obviously moved on. Or up.

As they approached the stairwell, something ahead of them, buried in shadow, moved. Avery motioned Drake back against the wall, and the two of them waited, listening. The soft tread of a footfall sounded against the floor.

Holding a finger against his lips, Avery sprang away from the wall, swinging around the corner, holding the Beretta so that the tac light cut across the hall.

"Whoa there cowboy," Tyler said, holding up her hands. "I'm on your side."

Avery lowered his weapon, and Drake joined them in the narrow hallway.

"You see anything suspicious in back?" he asked her.

"Nothing." She shook her head. "Place looks like it's been empty for a while. No trash in the bin. And nothing to indicate that anyone has been living here with any regularity."

"Same for us," Drake said. "Couple of rooms looked like vagrants might have moved in, but there's no sign of them now. In fact, from the looks of it, I'd say no one has been in here in one hell of a long time. You guys want to head up?" He motioned toward the stairs.

Avery nodded, and the three of them started up the steps, careful to keep from making noise as they climbed. Again they swung out into the hallway with guns at the ready, but when the silence stretched on, they lowered their weapons and continued to sweep through the rooms.

Like those on the first, the rooms here were empty too and, if possible, more derelict than the others, with only the occasional chair or desk to mark the fact that the building had once been occupied. Here, too, the wallpaper was peeling, the damp causing patches of mold to form along the line between the ceiling and the wall.

"Doesn't look like anyone has been here in a while," Drake offered. "Looks to me like we've been sent on a snipe hunt."

"The relevant question being whether that's by design or because Isaacs didn't make his meeting," Avery added. "Nash, you finding anything?"

"Not a damn thing," Nash reported, static accompanying him over the earpiece. "I've cleared the fourth floor, and I'm almost finished with the third. I'll meet you down there in a few."

"Roger that," Avery acknowledged, his mind churning as he

tried to make sense of the situation. "Harrison, you showing any activity on the street?"

"Negative. It's as quiet as a graveyard out here. Not a soul in sight."

"Fucking Isaacs," Drake mumbled. "Looks like he's playing us even in death."

"I don't know," Tyler said. "This whole thing feels more like something the Consortium would pull, if you ask me. This is their kind of game. Bait and switch. Always reminding us that they're one step ahead."

"Yeah, well if they're behind this," Drake posited, "then you can bet there's a reason."

"The only real question being what?"

"Don't know," Nash said, striding down the hallway. "But it seems to me, based on past experience, we'd be better off getting the hell out of here first and asking questions later."

Chapter 18

The pub was crowded. Clearly a popular neighborhood hangout. Sydney counted out the proper coins to pay for their dinner and then took the sack from the bartender and headed for the door. Outside a group of men stood with pints of bitter, smoking and arguing about the outcome of the soccer game on TV, the screen visible through the window.

Men were men no matter the country. It was only the sport that varied. Her father had always said that football was serious business. She smiled and turned the corner into the cobblestone alleyway that ran between the main street and the mews.

The air was cold and damp, swirling tendrils of mist making the alley seem almost sinister somehow. Silly how quickly one's imagination could get carried away. Ahead, lights burned bright in the upper floors of the restored carriage houses. Once upon a time, the mews had housed horses and grooms. But in later centuries, the masses had moved in, and the little stables had become grand town homes. Or at least nice ones.

Sydney pulled her coat closer as she turned into the lane, her eyes moving automatically to sweep the area. Looking for threats.

If nothing else she was a creature of habit. Her hand moved automatically to the small of her back where she kept her gun, but her fingers met only skin. She'd left the weapon on the table in the upstairs library of the flat.

Not that she needed it. She could actually see the lights from the flat now. And the dark sedan the British government had loaned them. Hannah had insisted on driving, reciting the mantra "right is left and left is right" the entire way. Not that Sydney blamed her. She'd never really gotten the hang of driving period, too much of her life spent in her father's diplomatic cars and limos. The Walkers had always had a driver.

Maybe when she got back to the States, she'd make a point of fine-tuning the skill.

Behind her, a dog barked, and something skittered along the pavement. She picked up her pace, the sound of laughter coming from an open window acting as a tonic for her jangled nerves. There had simply been too much going on. Too many narrow escapes. And now, if anyone was in danger, it was Avery.

Just the thought of him made her stomach quiver. The night they'd spent together had been beyond amazing. And the idea that a man like Avery had actually chosen her—well, it boggled the mind. She smiled again, her mind replaying the more intimate parts of the evening. The man definitely knew how to hit her sweet spots.

The dog barked again, and Sydney was immediately back on alert. In front of her, a shadow detached itself from behind a parked car. A man smoking a cigarette. He flicked it away, the tip glowing orange as it tumbled to the ground.

"Sydney Price?" the man's voice was deep and commanding.

She thought about running, but then held her ground, gripping the sack of food, her body tensing as she prepared to fight.

"I'm sorry to intrude. Your friend said you'd gone out to the pub."

She frowned, trying to process this newest piece of information, careful to keep her distance, the light from the safe house beckoning just up the street. "I'm sorry, do I know you?"

"My bad," the man said, the soft, southern vowels of his American accent carrying clearly now. "I should have introduced myself." He smiled, his teeth shining white in the dark of the mews. "Bradley Cramden. I'm with the State Department. I've come about your father."

Her alarm shifted quickly from fears for her safety to her fears about her father.

"Is he all right?"

"I'm afraid he's had a heart attack."

"Is he…" She sucked in a breath, unwilling to complete the thought.

"No. No." Bradley held up a hand in apology. "He's alive. But he's still in pretty bad shape. And so they sent me to find you."

"They?" Something in his voice seemed off suddenly, and she took a step backward, her fist tightening.

"The State Department. And the CIA. They tried to reach you through Langley. And they sent me here."

Definitely something not quite right. But she couldn't quite shake the idea that her father was sick and needed her. Still better to be careful.

"Who did you talk to at Langley?" she asked, looking for some kind of confirmation.

"I didn't talk to anybody. Way above my pay level." The man laughed, the sound echoing in the empty mews. "I'm afraid I'm just the messenger. But I'm supposed to take you to our offices, and from there, they'll get you on a flight to Vienna."

There was nothing in what he said that wasn't plausible. In fact, if he'd tried to name someone, she'd have been more concerned. No one in her business parted with names or information easily. Which either meant that Bradley was telling the truth, or was really good at playing the game.

"Thank you for coming for me," she said, inching around in an effort to keep him from blocking her path to the safe house and Hannah. "I just need to tell my friend you've found me. And grab my go-bag."

She didn't have a go-bag, but if he was who he said he was, he'd understand her hesitation.

"No problem," he smiled again. "I'll just walk with you." Before she could object, he'd fallen into step beside her. And as they passed through a pale sliver of light, she saw the gun glinting in his hand.

Acting on instinct alone, she whirled around, using her hand and leg as a weapon, the food sack sailing forgotten through the air. But the man had anticipated her movement, ducking away from her blow as his arms came around her, pulling her tight against his chest. She fought against him, trying to scream, but he pressed his fingers into her neck.

In seconds, her head was swimming as she struggled to breathe, and the last thought she had before slipping into blackness was that she should have told Avery how much she loved him.

* * *

"How the hell did you let this happen?" Avery knew he was yelling, and he also knew in some far-off corner of his brain that it wasn't going to do anyone any good, but he couldn't seem to stop himself. It was the only way he could maintain any semblance of control.

Sydney was missing. He'd only just found her, and now she was gone. Disappeared.

The only testament to her having been there at all was the remains of what was meant to have been hers and Hannah's dinner splattered all over the cobblestones.

"I had no reason to believe that she wasn't safe. The pub wasn't very far away. And no one was supposed to know we were here. And she was going crazy. Worrying about you." Hannah's face was pinched, her eyes wide behind her glasses. "Avery, if I'd known there was danger, I would never have let her go."

"I know." He sighed, sinking into a chair. "I didn't mean to take it out on you. It's not your fault. It's mine. I never should have left her on her own."

"Avery, she's a trained operative," Nash said. "She didn't need babysitters. And Hannah's right, there was no reason to believe that there was any kind of threat."

"Goddamned Consortium. We should have known the warehouse was a diversion. Finding the coordinates was just too easy."

"But they couldn't have known that Sydney would stay behind," Tyler offered.

"They might have, if they know CIA protocol," Drake said as Tyler glared at him, shaking her head. "Well, it's true. We've thought for a while that they might have someone on the inside. And if they do, then they could have figured out what our play would be."

"He's right." Avery pushed up from the chair, pacing instead in front of the flat's fireplace. "We might as well have given them a playbook. We followed protocol to the letter. Splitting up the team. Pulling rank with MI5. And then following those bastards as they led us on a merry chase, all the while planning to take Sydney."

"We don't know that it was the Consortium," Harrison said, his arm around Hannah, who was still looking shell-shocked.

"No, but it's a damn good guess," Drake argued.

"Consortium or not, we can be sure of one thing. This is definitely about me." Avery tipped back his head, pain ripping through him as he thought of the danger he'd put Sydney in. His falling in love with her had put a target on her back. "Everything that's happened. The altered photograph of Evangeline. Being lured back to Shrum's compound. The attack there. All of it was about me."

"Agreed," Nash said. "We've also got hard evidence to tie it all back to the Consortium as well. Which means that whatever the reason, they're gunning for you."

"And now they've got Sydney, and we haven't got shit." Avery dropped into the chair again, burying his face in his hands. He'd never felt so angry or so helpless. He wasn't the kind of man to sit and wait. And yet, without something to go on, there was nothing he could do.

"Actually," Hannah said, her voice still a little shaky, "I do have something. But I don't know if it will help."

"Anything you've got is better than where we are now."

"Okay." She nodded, moving to sit at her computer again. "I've been trying to find a link between Warner Stoltz and the man Gregor. Using our theory about Consortium members being tied to the arms trade, I ran names to see what might pop. And I got a hit. A man named Gregor Ivanovich. He's a Georgian national. Lives in Germany." She hit a button, and a face flashed up on the screen.

"Basically, he's a muscle man," she continued. "Security. Bodyguard. That kind of thing. Most recently working for a company out of Koln. BK Industries. It's a huge conglomerate. But they're heavily invested in the manufacturing of weapons."

"I've heard of them." Drake nodded. "One of the top producers in Europe. They even sell to the United States. But how do you know this Gregor is our man?"

"Couple of reasons." Hannah put up another photo. "Before going to work for BK, Gregor worked for an independent security company. More like mercenaries really. In fact, some of their members have even hit our watch lists. But the interesting part is that the security company also hired Warner Stoltz."

"So he was there at the same time as Gregor Ivanovich?" Tyler asked.

"Yes. And according to the records I found, they worked together quite a bit during that time."

"Is Stoltz still with the same company?" Harrison prompted.

"No. He left. Just after Gregor did."

"You said there were a couple of things. I don't suppose one of them is that Stoltz worked for BK."

"It's not that tidy, I'm afraid. But I did find out that Alain Dubois hired the company they worked for several times. Security for various functions he hosted. And it seems both Gregor and Warner were part of the deal."

"So we can connect both men to Dubois." Avery pushed aside his panic, trying to make the newest pieces of the puzzle fit.

"Yes," Hannah nodded. "And we know Dubois was a major player with the Consortium. But the best part is that one of the functions that he used them as security for was a benefit honoring the chairman of BK."

"Wait," Drake said, holding up a hand. "I know this one.

Michael Brecht, right? He's always in the papers. Guy's richer than God."

"Got it in one." Hannah shot a look at Avery. "I know it's not an answer but it's a start. And there's a little more. Gregor went to work for BK just after Dubois was killed. He started as security for Brecht and worked his way up to right-hand man."

"The pieces fit," Nash said. "Brecht certainly has the credibility and wherewithal to have pulled together something like the Consortium. And at least on the surface, there are some interesting connections. Any reason to suspect that he might be playing both sides of the weapons market? Legitimate and black?"

"There have been rumors. Unsubstantiated intel. But nothing definitive. On paper, the man is clean."

"If Michael Brecht is our man, then there's got to be a tie to me. And to Shrum. Clearly the man wants to hit me where it hurts. So it's got to be something that would have made him go after Evangeline and now Sydney."

"I haven't found the connection yet," Hannah said. "But I've got a gut feeling that it's there. This guy fits the profile of the kind of man arrogant enough to believe he could control the world's arms market by keeping countries destabilized. And he's also got the money and clout to recruit others of like mind. Add to that the connection to Gregor and Stoltz, both of whom are more than capable of killing people who outlive their usefulness."

"Like Isaacs," Drake added.

"Among others."

"I've got more information on Brecht," Harrison said, pulling up a recent photo of Brecht on his computer. "I have no idea if it'll help, but it can't hurt. Right?"

Avery moved so that he could see the screen as well as Harrison. "So what have you got?"

"The man's résumé definitely reads like a who's who of European industrial magnates. But he wasn't always rich. Started out on the wrong side of the German divide. Managed to work his way up in the communist hierarchy. Actually worked for a Soviet weapons manufacturer. But it wasn't until the wall came down that he came into his own. He started BK, which stands for Blitzkrieg, and never looked back. Capitalism was his kind of game."

"Yes, but there's still nothing to tie Brecht to me," Avery said. "What about family?"

Harrison typed something else into the computer, waited a moment, and then pulled up another picture of Brecht. This one when the man was much younger, standing in front of a bakery with a woman and a younger boy. "His father died when he was young. Mother remarried. This is a picture of Brecht, his mother, and his half brother. The bakery belonged to the stepfather."

"Prager." Avery read the name on the bakery, something stirring in his memory. "Is that the stepfather's name?"

"Yeah." Harrison nodded. "Manfred Prager. Michael never took his name. But his mother did. And, of course, his brother."

"What was the brother's name?" Avery's pulse was pounding now, memories of an operation years ago surfacing.

"Gerhardt," Harrison said. "Gerhardt Prager. But he died—"

"Sixteen years ago," Avery finished for him. "In Amsterdam. I know because I'm the one who killed him."

Chapter 19

Syd woke up with a start, her head aching and her muscles screaming. She was sitting on a chair, her hands tied behind her, her feet securely bound. From the little she could see, she was being held in some kind of a barn. The smell of oats, hay, and damp earth permeated the air. There was straw strewn across the ground and rough-hewn boards making up the walls.

Across the way, she could just make out the wooden slats of a stall, the soft sound of a whinny confirming her guess. In the far corner, she could see a saddle and bridle hanging from a large peg with an open barrel sitting just beneath them. Above her head, two huge hooks hung from rafters along with a large scythe and a double wooden yoke, the latter looking as if it hadn't been used in at least a century.

Some kind of loft stretched to her right, bisecting the arched roof and filled with rounded bales of hay. A single light, attached to the wall, gave the place a pale wash of light. And in the wall stretching up above the loft, she could see an open window, the night sky pitch-black. No stars. No moon.

No hope.

She shook her head, angry at the turn of her thoughts. There was always hope. Particularly now that she had Avery and his team on her side. Of course, there was the small problem of their not knowing where she was and who had taken her. But her money was still on A-Tac. And besides, it wasn't as if she was helpless.

All she had to do was figure a way out. Use her head. Her father was always saying he'd take brains over brawn. So now was the time to prove him right. Before her captors had the chance to use her abduction to manipulate her father.

Of course, it was also possible that this was about Avery. After all, someone had gone to quite a bit of trouble to lure him to Myanmar and set up the attack on Shrum's compound. But those same people had also tried to kidnap her. And she'd heard her father's name mentioned. So maybe it was about both men. Her father and Avery. The two men she loved most.

Well, she'd be damned if she was going to let them use her to hurt either one of them. After all, she wasn't exactly a helpless female. She twisted, trying to break her bonds. But the rope was nylon, and the more she struggled, the tighter the knots seemed to pull, the binding cutting into her wrists and palms.

Next she tried to work her feet free, but again the knots refused to budge. Maybe if she could lift up, she could slide her hands over the top of the chair. It wouldn't give her much, but it might allow her to at least pull herself out of the barn.

Using her feet to push upward, she tried sliding her arms along the back of the chair, ignoring the bite of splinters as she moved. But just as she thought she might be making a little headway, she felt her hands hit something hard. A brace in the back of the chair. The rope had been threaded through it. There was no way to pull herself free.

For a moment, defeat threatened to swamp her, but then she

thought about all the reasons she had to live. Most of them involving Avery. She'd only just found him, and she sure as hell wasn't going to give him up without a fight.

Using her body for leverage and her feet to guide her, she began to inch the chair forward, the odd hopping motion sending dust flying into the still air of the barn. Ignoring the pain from the ropes cutting into her ankles and the blood dripping down her wrists, she continued the combination. Hop—slide—hop—slide. Each movement taking her closer and closer to her objective, a small saw hanging with several other tools on a pegboard near the far wall.

It wasn't the best of plans, but at the moment, it was all she had. Hop—slide—hop—slide. She'd made it only about halfway when she heard a door behind her swing open, the creaking sound filling the barn as the horse in the stall stomped in protest. Heart pounding, Sydney frantically scanned the immediate area for some kind of weapon, the tools, unfortunately, still tantalizingly out of reach.

"Well done," a man said as he moved into the light. Fine-boned with straight blond hair, he was well dressed and, judging from the fine lines around his eyes, just past middle age. His smile was cold, his green eyes devoid of emotion. "You almost made five feet. Of course, judging from the blood on the ground, I'd have to say the price was rather high, especially since you managed to accomplish nothing."

If she could have called up enough saliva, she'd have spit at the bastard. But her mouth remained stubbornly dry. So she settled for glaring at him instead.

"Cat got your tongue?" the man taunted, his eyes narrowing, a hint of cruelty flashing there. "I'd have thought you'd be full of questions."

For a moment, she continued to stare at him defiantly, and then with a soft sigh, she capitulated the round. "What do you want with me?"

"With you personally, nothing," the man said. "As with most things in life, it's all about who you know. And in your case, I'd say you've made the wrong connections."

Behind him, just visible among the shadows, two men with guns stood guard. Not the best of odds, but if she could keep him talking, maybe she could still figure a way out.

"I don't know what you're talking about," she bluffed, not willing to give him anything without a fight—even information.

"Why am I not surprised? They teach you how to handle this kind of thing at Langley, don't they? How to hold out and keep from talking? Only you see, I already have all the information I need. For instance, I know that your father will do almost anything in order to guarantee your safety. And I also know that, if he were asked to do so, Avery Solomon would die for you. Men are so predictable in that way."

She swallowed a curse, kicking out with her feet in the hopes of at least causing him some pain. But he stepped easily out of her reach, a smile twisting on his face.

She struggled for balance and then lifted her gaze to meet his. "You seem to know everything about me. It seems only fair that I know something about you." She held his gaze, not allowing herself to flinch when he reached out to caress her cheek.

"Such a lovely woman. And a spitfire to boot. I can see why Avery loves you. You're very much like his wife."

"What the hell do you know about Evangeline?"

"I know that if she'd lived, she'd have left him. She wasn't the type to suffer overly protective men. Particularly Neanderthals like Avery."

"You have no idea what you're talking about. Avery and Evangeline loved each other. And if she'd lived, they'd still be together."

"And you'd be out in the cold."

He was toying with her. Playing a game with rules only he knew. But she wasn't going to give him the satisfaction of playing. "You still haven't told me who you are." She sat back, feeling calmer. Knowing that the only chance she had to escape was to stay alert and not let him manipulate her emotions.

He studied her for a moment and then shrugged. "My name is Michael. Michael Brecht."

"And you killed Evangeline." She'd said it to keep him off balance, but the minute the words were out of her mouth, she knew they were true.

Anger flashed in his eyes, but just as quickly was gone, replaced with a cold mask of indifference. Whoever Michael Brecht was, he hid his emotions deep. "I didn't kill her."

"Maybe not directly, but you were responsible nevertheless. You're the one who ordered Isaacs to build that bomb. And Kamaal to set it off." Again she had the sense that she'd struck a blow. But Brecht still held all the cards.

"You know more than I expected. I suppose I shouldn't have underestimated you. Not that it matters, you're only a means to an end."

"And when you've finished using me, you'll kill me." Again she'd clearly shocked him with her directness.

"That depends on your father. But before we get to that, I'm going to see about that trade I mentioned earlier. Your life for Avery's."

"But surely the pain is more powerful if you kill me and leave him to live with the loss."

"Been there, done that," Brecht waved a hand in dismissal. "Avery's been a thorn in my side for too long now. First he took away the most important person in my life. And now he's a threat to everything I've been trying to accomplish."

"You're talking about the Consortium."

Brecht's gaze raked across her face, his eyes narrowed as he studied her. "As usual, Avery has chosen well. Perhaps when this is over, I'll have to try to win you over myself."

"Not a chance in hell."

"Never say never, my dear. But first things first." Brecht pulled a cell phone from his pocket and dialed, his gaze still resting on her face as he waited for the other party to pick up. There was an audible click, and then he hit the button for speaker phone.

"Avery Solomon?"

"Who the hell is this?" Even over the phone lines his voice had the ability to soothe her.

"Unless I've totally misread your little band of miscreants, I'm guessing you already know that. Surely pretty Hannah has put it together by now."

There was a pause, and Sydney could almost feel Avery's anger arcing from cell tower to cell tower. "Look, Brecht," he said finally. "Whatever is going on here, it's between you and me. Let Sydney go."

"I can't blame you for trying, but I hardly think I'm going to fold when I've got the winning hand. But you're right. This is between you and me. So I'll give you a chance to right the wrong. Be an honorable man. Your life for hers. It's as simple as that."

"Just tell me where to come."

"I'll text you the coordinates. But make no mistake, if you don't come alone, or if I see any indication that your people are trying to back you up, I'll kill her. One wrong move, Solomon, and she's dead. Am I making myself clear?"

"Crystal," Avery said, his big voice filling the barn, giving her strength and, despite the reality of the situation, hope. "But before we have a deal, let me speak to her. I need to know that she's all right."

Again Brecht hesitated, and then with a sigh, he held the phone to Sydney's ear. "Avery?" she said, hating that her voice sounded shaky.

"Sweetheart, are you all right?"

"I'm fine," she said, forcing herself to sound calmer. "But you can't come for me. He'll kill you if you do. Please, Avery, if you love me, don't come."

"It's because I love you that I'm going to do it. There's no way I'm leaving you there with that bastard."

"But I can't...I don't..." she started but stopped, tears filling her eyes. "I won't let you die for me."

"Well then, sweetheart, we'll just have to figure out another option."

Brecht jerked the phone away, teeth clenched, anger flashing in his eyes. "Believe me when I tell you, Avery, that you're all out of options. I promise, I've seen to that. So come quickly. And come alone. Or she dies."

He hit the disconnect button and dropped the phone back into his pocket. Then he reached out to run a finger along the line of her jaw. She jerked back, almost upsetting the chair, and he laughed. "I'm afraid, my dear, that you've put your money on the wrong team. But don't worry, there's still time to change your mind."

"Not likely," she spat. "And besides, you're not going to kill me. At least not yet. You've already said that you need me so that you

can manipulate my father. And if he hasn't already, Avery will figure that out."

"Ah yes, but you see the beauty of a man like Avery Solomon is
that he's predictable. Even if he believes there's a chance I'm bluff-
ing, he won't risk your life on it. He'll be noble to the very end."
Brecht stepped back, eyes sparkling with malice. "You know, if it
weren't so damned enjoyable, I might even feel sorry for him."

Sydney started to speak but held her tongue. There was nothing to be gained in tipping her hand. But clearly Michael Brecht
didn't know Avery Solomon as well has he thought he did.

* * *

"I'm here." Avery walked into the barn, hands raised, palms
turned upward. Everything depended on Brecht believing he'd
truly come in alone. "Where's Sydney?"

"She's safe," Michael Brecht said, stepping into a pool of light
cast from a bare bulb on the wall.

"I want to see her," Avery insisted, adrenaline coursing
through his veins. There was no reason to believe that Sydney was
dead. Because of her father, she was more valuable alive. No matter how much Brecht hated Avery. But fear worked its way up his
spine anyway, the thought of losing her more than he could bear.

Brecht tipped his head to one side, and a second light came on,
this one over a stall. Beneath it, Sydney sat, gagged and bound to
a chair. Avery took a step forward, but Brecht waved him still.

"Not so fast. I need to be sure you're unarmed."

"I told you I would be," Avery snapped, his fear getting the
better of him. But over Brecht's shoulder, he could see Sydney
nodding slightly, her green eyes telegraphing that she was just as
angry as he was. And instantly he felt better. Sydney was a strong

woman. And in the short time he'd known her, they'd already been through worse than this. All he had to do was keep Brecht distracted.

"All right." He held his arms out from his sides. "Have a look, if you don't believe me." Brecht signaled two men who'd been standing by the door. The first kept his gun trained on Avery while the second stepped forward. Gregor. Avery recognized him from Hannah's photos.

"Search him." Brecht waved a hand, his gesture imperious, his expression smug. Bastard thought he had the upper hand.

Gregor nodded, running his hands none too gently down Avery's torso, arms, and legs. Carefully searching his ears, face, and mouth as well. "He's clean. No weapons and no communications devices."

"Nice to know that you follow orders as easily as you give them," Brecht noted as two more armed men walked into the barn. "Any sign of Mr. Solomon's minions?"

"No, sir," the man replied. "He appears to have come on his own."

"What about his vehicle?" Brecht asked, his gaze darting from his man to Avery and then back again.

"A jeep. The GPS and radio had already been disabled, and we checked thoroughly for any other kind of tracking device. It's clean."

"Destroy it. And then keep a close watch on our perimeter. Despite Mr. Solomon's apparent cooperation, it's never a good idea to trust a gift horse." For a moment, Brecht's attention was centered on his men. And as the second group of men retreated, Avery took the opportunity to shift his position toward Sydney. They were only a few feet apart now, but Brecht still stood between them.

"You seem to have thought of everything," Avery said, more to keep him talking than because he cared. All he needed was a little more time.

Over Brecht's shoulder, Sydney's gaze collided with his, and a million unsaid things were communicated with a single look. It was as if they were connected in some kind of cosmic way. Avery had never felt this way about another woman. Not even Evangeline. And his gut clenched at the thought that Sydney had come up on Brecht's radar only because of her association with him. If he managed to get them out of this in one piece, he fully intended to spend the rest of his life making it up to her.

"I didn't get where I am by neglecting details," Brecht was saying, thankfully not noticing their brief exchange.

"Heading up the Consortium, you mean."

"That"—he shrugged—"and other things. You've no idea how many pies I have a finger in."

"We have more information than you'd think. Certainly enough to have thwarted several of your attempts to upend peace accords and throw off political balance."

"All the talks," Brecht said, "they're nothing more than false hope. Sooner or later it will all come unraveled. Human nature is to conquer and destroy. Anything else is simply a fool's game."

"But this isn't about the Consortium, is it? At least not at its core. This is about you and me."

"Beyond anything you can possibly conceive." Brecht's face contorted, rage turning it red. Hatred flashing in his eyes. "But now, finally, Gerhardt will have peace."

"Gerhardt is dead. Whatever peace there is in that, he found sixteen years ago."

"When you killed him."

"It was self-defense. The kid drew a gun. He didn't give me a choice."

"There's always a choice, Mr. Solomon. You just made the wrong one."

"Or you did. As I remember it, Gerhardt was there representing the seller. A last-minute replacement due to a conflict. So instead, it was his job to sell thirty-five Soviet cruise missiles. We'd been tracking them for months. And when word got out that they'd surfaced, we set up the sting. Gerhardt's die was cast the minute you sent him in to make the sale."

"My brother was my life. And you're right, I did send him in. But you're the one who pulled the trigger."

"And your guilt is what's driven you all these years."

"Make no mistake, Mr. Solomon. It's not guilt that's driving me. It's hatred. For you and for all the others like you. Sanctimonious pricks who believe they're serving the greater good. The only people you serve are yourselves and your need for the next adrenaline high. You're modern-day cowboys, and people like my brother get caught in the crossfire."

"Then why the hell did you send him into that kind of situation?"

"Because he begged me." Bitterness filled Brecht's voice, his pain palpable. Above him, in the shadows of the loft, Avery saw a flash of movement. "And I never could say no."

"And so all of this—" Avery waved a hand as if a gesture could encompass it all. "Evangeline. The Consortium. Sydney. This is because of one bad decision?"

Brecht roused himself from his memories, pulling a gun. "This is because of you. You killed Gerhardt. You took him from me. And so I've taken everything from you."

"That you have. But you promised you'd let Sydney go, if I came. So now is the time to honor that promise."

"Ah, but there is no honor among thieves, surely you knew that much." He leveled the gun, pointing it at Sydney. Terror clawing at his gut, Avery launched himself at her, tackling the chair, driving both it and her to the ground, covering her with his body, mindless of the barrage of bullets exploding around him.

For what seemed like an eon, he held her, praying that he'd been in time, that she was still breathing. Bullets ricocheted everywhere. He could hear the reverb as it bounced off the barn walls.

And then everything was quiet. In his peripheral vision, he could see Michael Brecht, gun still clutched in lifeless fingers.

Slowly, almost afraid to breathe, Avery moved back, his hands reaching for Sydney, fumbling with her bonds, and then she was in his arms. Warm. Alive. His heart started to beat again. And he held her close, content for the moment just to feel the rhythm of her breathing.

"Hey, I know you're happy to see each other again," Drake's voice broke through the silence. "But, really, I'd think you'd find a moment to thank the cavalry."

Drake stepped into the first pale rays of dawn as they slanted through the barn. Behind him stood Harrison and Hannah. Nash and Tyler dropped down from their places in the loft. And the team stood quietly surveying the damage. Brecht was dead. As were most of his men. A few, like Gregor, had been taken captive. The backup men from MI5 were already moving them out to be transferred for interrogation.

It was a win. And hopefully a death blow for the Consortium.

"Are you okay?" Sydney asked, pushing back from his embrace to search his face.

"I've never been better," he said. "It's finally over. Brecht is dead. And we're alive and we're together. And I love you more than you can possibly imagine."

"Well, if you like, you could try to show me." Her lips curved into a sexy smile, her eyes full of invitation.

"I don't know, it could take a while." Behind him Drake cleared his throat, but Avery just smiled, his eyes never leaving hers.

"Not a problem," she whispered, leaning close, her lips brushing against his, "thanks to you and your team, we've got all the time in the world."

Epilogue

Sydney looked out over the large group of guests assembled in the college's elegant ballroom. It had been a marvelous wedding, and the reception was turning into quite a party. Dignitaries talking with spooks. Desk jockeys mixing with people who served on the front lines. Politicians making nice with bureaucrats. Even the vice president was here somewhere. Although Sydney hadn't voted for the woman.

In truth, there were enough dignitaries present to make for a politically star-studded event. Many of them had been invited because of her father, but there was also a large group attending to honor Avery.

She glanced over at her husband of exactly two hours. He was deep in conversation with Drake and his wife, Madeline, Drake waving his hands as he told some story or another. Probably something to do with baseball. As if he'd felt her gaze, Avery looked up, his smile contagious, his eyes telegraphing his love. Sydney felt her heart swell with pride. She'd never known she could love someone so completely. And to think that she'd been given the chance to share her life with him. The idea excited and humbled her all at the same time.

Farther across the room, her father and mother were talking with Nash and his wife, Annie. Between them, their son, Adam, was looking slightly bored, but incredibly dapper in his tuxedo. Annie laughed at something Sydney's father said, and she swelled with pride again. This was her family now. Her parents, and her new friends from A-Tac.

"It was a beautiful wedding," Hannah said, handing her a glass of champagne. For once, she looked almost subdued, and most definitely gorgeous, dressed in the pewter satin gown that had been chosen for Sydney's bridesmaids, her usually wild hair pulled into a chic chignon.

"You and Harrison should jump right in," Sydney teased. "I promise the water's fine."

"While I applaud you and Avery taking the plunge"—she laughed—"I can assure you Harrison and I are just fine. We've already made all the commitment we'll ever need. For us, it's enough just to be together."

"As long as you're happy." Sydney smiled, lifting her glass as Tyler, also clad in gray satin, walked over to join them.

"I think Owen and Tucker are going to duke it out. Apparently the bar has the baseball game on, and Owen wants to change it to soccer. I told them they should both be over here with the bride and groom. But who knows if they'll listen." Tucker was Drake's brother, and Owen, a former MI6 agent, was Tyler's husband. And, in the way of small world connections, it turned out also a friend of Tim's.

He'd joined with Avery in working to find out the real truth about Tim's death. And in the end, it turned out that Shrum had been right. It had been Wai Yan. And now, thanks to the joint operation, he'd been apprehended and was being held at some undisclosed British stronghold. Hopefully, selling out his compatriots in an effort to save his miserable life.

Gregor Ivanovich had also proven quick to fold. It had been only a matter of days before he'd broken, giving A-Tac the information they needed to take down the Consortium once and for all. There were probably still other members out there, but the organization had been crippled from the top down. And with additional investigation, Sydney had no doubt that any outliers would be identified and captured as well.

"Tyler said we have to behave," Owen groused, breaking into Sydney's thoughts as he and Tucker arrived, also carrying glasses of champagne.

"It wasn't just Tyler." Alexis Flynn, Tucker's wife, grinned. "I'm sorry they're not behaving."

"It's a party," Nash protested as he and Annie joined the group. "We're not supposed to behave."

"I'm just sorry Lara and Rafe couldn't be with us," Hannah said. "You'll love her when you finally get to meet her."

"I know I will." Sydney nodded, meaning every word. All of Avery's friends had accepted her without question. Making her feel as if she'd been a part of their lives a lot longer than the four months she'd actually known them.

"They're supposed to be here next week," Harrison said, slipping an arm around Hannah. "Although she's technically not supposed to travel with the baby." They'd just adopted a little girl from Nicaragua and had been forced to miss the wedding. "She swears that she's going to make you go through the whole thing again."

"Not that I'd mind a bit." Avery's deep voice surrounded Sydney like a caress. And she leaned back into his arms as he pulled her into his embrace.

"What I think we need," Simon Kincaid, a former A-Tac operative and current Sunderland professor, said, "is a toast." He and his wife, J.J., passed out additional glasses of champagne to the assembled company.

"Yes, definitely a toast," Madeline agreed, as she and Drake took champagne from the tray.

"To my wife," Avery said, lifting his glass. "It's been a long time since I felt this happy."

"And I can't remember ever feeling this loved." For just a moment, it was only the two of them. And Sydney relished the fact that, as long as they were together, anything was possible.

Then she widened her smile. "And to all of you." She lifted her glass higher, surrounded by her new family, people she'd come to care about so dearly. "It seems that sometimes, the good guys really do save the day."

Avery nodded his approval, his proud gaze encompassing his team as they all clinked glasses. "To A-Tac."

Have you missed any of A-Tac's adventures? See where the series started with this excerpt from *Dark Deceptions*.

See the next page for an excerpt from

Dark Deceptions.

Chapter 3

There's got to be a mistake," Nash said, his mind still reeling. "There's no way Annie would sign on for that kind of thing."

"People change." Avery shrugged.

"Someone want to tell me who the hell Annie Gallagher is?" Drake asked, his dark gaze falling on Nash.

He tried to find words, but couldn't, his brain still trying to make sense of the idea that Annie was playing for the other team.

"She was Nash's partner before he came to A-Tac. A trained assassin. One of the best, if rumors are to be believed," Tyler said, coming to his rescue. She and Avery were the only ones who knew just how much Annie's defection had cost him. "Nash and Annie worked special ops. Mainly in the former Eastern Bloc. Some of the Company's most dangerous missions."

"So what happened?" Hannah asked.

"She jumped ship in the middle of a mission," Nash said, fighting against his anger and the memories. "Fucking disappeared. And I damn near died because of it."

"Maybe something happened to her," Emmett offered. "I

mean, our line of work doesn't exactly lead to winning popularity contests."

"That's what I thought at first," Nash said, his tone laced with bitterness. "And believe me when I say that I explored every possibility. But everything I managed to discover only underscored the idea that her disappearance was planned. Annie was always good at details."

"Sometimes there are good reasons to jump ship," Drake said, eyes narrowed, "but that doesn't excuse her leaving you to die. What the hell happened?"

"Long story." Nash shook his head. "But the short version is that we got cornered in a building in Lebanon. Saida. My last mission before leaving to join A-Tac. Anyway, Annie and I got separated and I got pinned down in the firefight. There was an explosion and half my shoulder got ripped off. I was trapped, but she never came back. Just left me there to die."

"But you made it out okay," Tyler said, her eyes dark with anger.

"Yeah, I did. No thanks to Annie."

"She betrayed your trust," Emmett said.

"Which shouldn't be all that surprising. Hell, it's part and parcel of the gig." Drake grimaced. "They train us to doubt everything we see and hear. Trust nothing and no one."

"Except your partner. If you can't trust him or her, you might as well pack it in." Lara frowned, shooting a look in Jason's direction.

"Maybe I just picked the wrong person," Nash sighed, shaking his head to clear his thoughts. Whatever the hell kind of relationship he'd had with Annie, it had imploded in Lebanon. Along with any loyalty he might owe her. "So, Avery, what have you got that makes you think it's her?"

"Intel picked up three separate references to Titian while picking through the chatter," Avery said. "Two of them directly referencing what we believe to be plans for the assassination."

"Titian as in the painter?" Jason asked, typing furiously on his laptop.

"Indirectly." Avery nodded. "Annie has red hair. Titian was her code name."

"Bit of a blinding glimpse of the obvious." Drake frowned.

"Sometimes the best way to hide is in plain sight." Emmett shrugged.

"Yeah, but in this case it doesn't make sense. Annie's disappearance was without sanction. That means that she's persona non grata as far as the CIA is concerned. So surfacing now using an old CIA code name would set off all kinds of alarm bells." Nash shook his head, frustration cresting. "I think it's far more likely that someone's playing us. Trying to make us believe it's Annie, when, in fact, it's not."

"The possibility occurred to me, too," Avery said, his expression, as usual, masking any emotion. "But there's more." He picked up a remote and pressed a button, the screen behind him filling with the photograph of a man entering a small hotel. "This picture was taken yesterday afternoon in D.C. The man is Emanuel Rivon, a Bolivian national with known terrorist ties. He operates a coffee conglomerate and uses it to cover travel in and out of questionable countries. Including Pakistan."

"Has he been specifically linked to Ashad?" Lara asked.

"Not specifically, no." Avery shook his head. "But intel can establish that he does business with people who do have ties to the group."

"Guilt by association," Drake said to no one in particular.

"Sometimes it's all we've got. But in this case we can verify that Rivon met recently with two suspected Ashad sympathizers. Both Pakistani and both alleged to have strong ties with radical Islam. This photo was taken about sixteen hours after that meeting."

"I assume you have something connecting Rivon to Annie?" Lara asked.

Avery nodded, hitting the remote again. The screen filled with another photograph, same hotel, but this time the camera had captured the image of a woman. Nash struggled to breathe, long-sequestered emotions threatening to overwhelm him. Despite the passing years, Annie looked just the same. The fall of her hair, the slant of her eyes, even the small scar that bisected her left eyebrow—a souvenir from a particularly incendiary operation—nothing had changed.

"This photo was taken fifteen minutes after Rivon entered the building. If we hadn't been watching him, we'd probably never have seen this."

"It could be coincidence," Nash started, trailing off as he realized just how delusional he sounded. Annie was clearly a part of something big. And the fact that she'd fucked him over eight years ago only gave credence to the idea.

"In our business there's no such thing," Drake said, his expression hard, as he stared at the photograph.

"Is there anything more?" Tyler asked.

"More chatter. This time a veiled reference to a meeting between Titian and El Halcón."

"The Falcon," Emmett repeated. "Rivon's code name?"

"Exactly." Avery nodded, his expression harsh.

"And if you play connect the dots," Drake said, "you end up with Rivon hiring Annie to do Ashad's dirty work."

"Makes sense." Hannah shrugged. "With security what it is, it's a hell of a lot easier to hire someone already in country. Especially if said person is a professional assassin."

The label hung in the air, no one willing to look at Nash.

"So you think Annie's turned mercenary?" Nash said, his jaw clenching as he fought his anger. It was a reasonable assumption, but that didn't make it any easier to swallow.

"She wouldn't be the first." Jason shrugged.

"I don't know," he said, frowning as he tried to sort through the facts. "Don't you think it's a little suspect that she's showing her hand after all these years? Usually when people fall off the grid, they go out of their way to stay that way. Meeting with a known terrorist in the middle of D.C. is like waving a red flag."

"Or maybe she's just lost her edge," Lara said. "It's been a long time."

"You don't know Annie." Nash shook his head, anger mixing with frustration.

"But you do," Avery replied, his tone brooking no argument. "Which is exactly why the boys in Virginia dropped this in our backyard. They want you to spearhead the effort to bring Annie Gallagher down."

* * *

Annie paced in front of the hotel window, the traffic below indicating that it was rush hour in Baltimore. Time had lost all meaning, her every waking moment occupied with thoughts of finding her son. It had been almost thirty-seven hours since Adam had disappeared.

Less than two days. But it felt like years. The kidnappers had made their instructions clear. A phone call that had sent her across the country to D.C. and a meeting with a man named Emanuel Rivon.

It was dangerous coming out into the open after so many years, but she hadn't had a choice. The kidnappers had made it clear that there would be no negotiation. And that they were watching. Any attempt to contact the authorities, particularly the CIA, would result in Adam's death.

Not that she was tempted to go that route. She wasn't foolish enough to believe anyone from her old life would step in to help her now. For all practical purposes, black ops agents operated off the radar. And once they'd ceased to be useful, they ceased to exist, all ties with the past severed irrevocably. In return for her safety and her freedom, she'd agreed to a cover story that painted her a deserter.

It was for the greater good. At least that's what she'd been told. But now, standing here waiting for Rivon's call, she wondered if she hadn't made a bargain with the devil. In trying to save her son, she'd opened the door to a far more hideous danger.

So far they hadn't allowed her to speak with Adam. The only proof she had that he was still alive was a grainy photograph Rivon had given her. She picked up the picture for something like the thousandth time, studying every angle, looking for something—anything—that would give her some idea where they were holding him.

But the generic room gave nothing away.

She clenched her fists and stared at the PDA on the nightstand, willing it to ring or signal an incoming text message. Rivon had given her the phone at their meeting. Untraceable, it was no doubt rigged to track her movements as well. Although she hated the idea, she couldn't ditch it. It was her only link with Adam's kidnappers. Rivon had said they'd call her when everything was finalized.

He'd also promised a video call from Adam.

But so far...nothing.

She blew out a breath and leaned her forehead against the cold glass of the window. Life below her went on without so much as a pause. It was as if the universe were completely unaware of the nightmare she'd been thrown into.

Rivon hadn't exactly been a font of information. He hadn't even told her who it was he was working for. But clearly it was someone who knew who she was. Who she'd been. Someone who knew that taking Adam was the only way to pull her back into the game.

She fought against a sob, knowing that this was no time for emotion. She had to keep a clear head. Figure out where they were holding her son and find a way to get him out. And failing that, she'd have to follow through with their demands.

It meant crossing a line, but the choice was an easy one. Adam was her son. And if necessary she'd sacrifice her life for him. Or someone else's. Rivon had made that much perfectly clear.

She sighed, a shiver working its way up her spine.

It wasn't as if she'd never killed anyone. But in the past, she'd always believed she was working on the side of right. Fighting against corruption and evil. Making the world a safer place for children like Adam.

Maybe it had all been bullshit. Maybe there was no right or wrong. At least not in any absolute kind of way. The world was a dangerous place. And her involvement with the darker side of espionage was the only reason she was standing in a seedy hotel room praying for word from her son. All she knew for certain was that she'd do whatever it took to make sure that Adam was freed. Securing his release was the only thing that mattered.

She still had no idea who the target would be. Someone of

great importance, Rivon had said. A major player. A roadblock in the continuing battle to bring America to its knees.

She sank down on the end of the bed, desperation threatening all rational thought. Nothing had changed. It was the same war. Different opponents maybe. But still the same fight. And her son was caught in the middle of it.

Beside her the phone rang, and heart pounding, she snatched it off the bed, fumbling with the buttons in her rush to answer.

"Hello?" She held her breath, waiting. "Adam, is that you?"

"No, Ms. Gallagher. I'm afraid it's not your son."

"Rivon." The word came out more a curse than a name. "I want to speak to Adam."

"In good time. But there are a few things we need to discuss first."

She wondered if it was possible to hate anyone as much as she did this man. "So speak."

"It's almost time for you to make your move. And so I've been instructed to reveal the target."

"Aren't you worried that I'll tell someone?"

"Not particularly," he said, his tone smug. "You're more than aware of what would happen if you were to try to bring in outside help."

She sighed, knowing there was little point in arguing. Better to play along and keep alert. She needed to talk to Adam. "So who is it you want me to take out?"

"Spoken like a consummate professional." He laughed. "The target is an official with the U.N. Blake Dominico."

"The U.S. ambassador?" She tried but couldn't keep the dismay out of her voice. Not only was the man a patriot, he was probably, thanks to his often extreme views on eradicating the country's enemies, one of the most protected men in the country. "You're asking the impossible."

"That's why we have you. Your reputation precedes you."

"I haven't been a part of that world in years. And even then I wasn't operating on my own. I don't have the resources to pull something like this off by myself."

"I think you're underestimating your abilities, Ms. Gallagher. And besides, you've got more resources than you realize. Which is why I want you to go to New York and survey the situation. Then when you've come up with a plan, we'll see that you get whatever it is you need to make it happen."

"I'm not sure you have access to the kinds of resources that might be necessary. Blueprints, surveillance equipment, entrance codes, not to mention weaponry. Since 9/11, access to U.N. diplomats has become increasingly difficult. Particularly at the Secretariat."

"Yes, but Dominico doesn't spend every waking hour at the General Assembly. You'll find a way, Ms. Gallagher. After all, we have Adam. And it would be a shame for his life to end so soon. Wouldn't you agree?"

Blind rage threatened to overtake all rational thought, but she clenched the phone until the plastic cut into her fingers, the sharp bite of pain pulling her back from the edge. "I won't do anything more until I see my son. I need to know that he's okay." She paused, sucking in a breath of air, as her mind considered the unthinkable. "That he's still alive."

"You're not really in any position to be making demands," Rivon said. "But as it happens, we're prepared for you to speak with your son as soon as we've finished here."

"So what else do I need to know? You've made your objective crystal clear."

"I'll be texting a file with information and final instructions within the hour," he said, ignoring her open hostility.

"What about transportation? It'll be difficult to stay under the radar if I have to use my credit cards."

"All of that has been arranged. You'll receive everything you need."

"And if I don't? How can I contact you?" It was worth a try. A phone number would be the quickest route to tracking him down.

"You can't. At least not by any direct method. But again, arrangements have been made, and as I just said, you'll be apprised of the details very soon."

"Whatever," she said, her impatience growing by the second. "Let me talk to Adam."

"As you wish." The line went dead. And for a moment she panicked, fearing Rivon's promise had been nothing more than empty words, but two minutes later the phone signaled an incoming video. And holding her breath, Annie waited for the call to connect.

"Mommy?" Adam's face swam into view, blurred as much by her tears as by the quality of transmission.

"I'm here, baby. I'm right here." She leaned closer to the picture, as if in doing so she could somehow physically connect with her child. "Are you all right?"

"I think so." He nodded, his little face looking older than it should. "At first I was really scared. But there's a nice man here. He has a Wii. And we've been playing Super Smash Brothers. It's really cool." He paused, his chin quivering. "But I want to come home."

"I know, sweetie. And I'm doing everything I can to make that happen."

He nodded again. "Come soon, Mommy. Please."

Tears ran down her cheeks in earnest, her heart threatening to shatter. "I will, Adam. I promise. And in the meantime, you be brave."

"Like Daddy?"

"Like your daddy." She nodded, wondering for the millionth time why she'd made the man seem so much larger than life.

"He was really brave, right?"

"Yes," she said, frustration and anger blending with agony. "And so are you. Just hang in there, baby. I love you."

"I love you, too." He nodded.

"Everything's going to be okay. I swear it is. We'll be home before you know it."

"Can we have hot dogs?"

Annie felt a bubble of laughter but before she could say anything the screen went blank. Adam was gone.

"Hello?" she said, her voice cracking with emotion. "Adam?"

"He's no longer on the line," a disembodied voice said.

"When can I talk to him again?" she asked, desperation mixing with dread.

"When you've accomplished your objectives. I need for your focus to be complete."

"You have to know that I can't do anything well, knowing my son is in danger."

"Don't be ridiculous. You're a professional, Ms. Gallagher," the tinny voice said.

"That was a hell of a long time ago."

"Just get the job done." The connection went dead and Annie stood staring down at the phone. For one second, she considered forsaking common sense and calling in help. She and Nash might be estranged, but he'd never let her hang in the wind. Especially if he grasped the true significance of the situation. Even as she had the thought, she rejected it. She'd reached out to him once before, and he'd turned her down flat.

And besides, even if for some reason he did agree to help, she still didn't trust the CIA. At least not with her son. His death would be viewed as nothing more than collateral damage, the primary objective being to take out the threat, no matter the cost.

No. She couldn't risk asking for help. Nash was a Company man to the core. He'd proven that in no uncertain terms eight years ago. Which meant she was in this alone. And she'd find a way to save her son. Even if it meant killing an innocent man.

About the Author

Bestselling author Dee Davis worked in association management before turning her hand to writing. Her highly acclaimed first novel, *Everything in Its Time*, was published in July 2000. Since then, among others, she's won the Booksellers' Best, Golden Leaf, Texas Gold, and Prism awards, and been nominated for the National Readers' Choice Award, the Holt Medallion Award, and two RT Reviewers' Choice Awards. When not sitting at the computer writing, she spends her time exploring Manhattan with her husband, daughter, and Cardigan Welsh corgi.

You can learn more at:

DeeDavis.com

Twitter @deedavis

Facebook.com/deedavisbooks

CPSIA information can be obtained
at www.ICGtesting.com
Printed in the USA
FFOW04n0900130117
31284FF

9 781455 575305